MURDER, SHE DID IT

A Murder, She Wrote parody

HUDSON TAYLOR

Murder, She Did It

Copyright 2019 by Hudson Taylor

Books by Hudson Taylor

<u>Ethel Cunningham mysteries</u>

The Priest Wore One Green Sock

Killer Workout

Death Of A Christmas Tree Man

New Year's Eve Kill (short story)

New York Rents Can Be Murder

Island Of The Dolls

Salsa Hot, Murder Cold

<u>Murder, She Wrote parodies</u>

Murder, She Did It

Murder, She Tried A Brazilian Wax

The House By The Graveyard:

A Provincetown Ghost Story

Gentlemen Prefer Murder:

Marilyn Monroe Mysteries

Murder, at the Hair Salon:

Golden Girls parody mystery

4

MURDER,
SHE DID IT

HUDSON
TAYLOR

<u>Chapter One</u>

Mort Metzger took off his cowboy hat and used it to wipe his sweaty forehead. As the sheriff of Cabot Cove, Maine. He'd had more murders in a month than when he was a police officer in New York City, so much for transferring to a small New England town where the only murder was supposed to happen to the wildlife.

Gypsy Rose plopped herself down in front of Mort's desk like the very act of sitting was a bother. Through make-up smudged tears, she told him again how she didn't kill local fisherman, Clive Banning. He rarely met murderers who said they did the dirty deed, and even then, when they went to trial, they all cried innocence.

"I told you, sheriff, I was home watching The Real Housewives of New Brunswick, New Jersey. There is no way I could have thrown Clive into the lobster tank, I don't even like seafood."

Kips Seafood Shack was one of Cabot Cove's best restaurants and proudly bragged on many signs about its large tank that you could jump into and catch your lobster. The sign was a gimmick and luckily no one had ever tried to jump into the bacteria-infested tank except old Piccadilly Pete, and with only one ear, many thought the man had suffered enough and let him do as he pleased.

"I'm growing impatient with your lies, young lady, and after finding poor Clive, I swear it will hurt like hell when I go in for their lobster special tomorrow, but as my wife always tells me in bed, a deal is a deal"

"I didn't do it!"

"The evidence against you is top-notch, sister. Clive's open wall office on the second floor overlooked the lobster tank. When he turned his back on you, you hit him with the brass bowling ball pin he had on his desk and pushed him into the tank like he was fish food. Doc Hazlitt said the hit on the head and drowning led to his death."

As another officer held her back, Gypsy Rose cursed like a drunk Rap singer.

The door flew open and in walked writer and part-time sleuth, Jessica Fletcher.

"My dear, that kind of language will get you nowhere but the gutter."

"Hello, Mrs. F, I'm afraid Gypsy Rose is still saying she's innocent." Mort raised his eyebrow.

"Oh, you, poor child. I think you are just confused." Soft music seemed to play from nowhere, "Remember, you found out that Clive had stolen your house away from your family when your father was dying in the hospital? I'll never forget the look on your eleven-year-old face at your father's funeral when Clive told you to hit the road because he owned your house and even the bike you rode on. It broke my heart to see all the dirt blowing on you as our limos sped by, and you walking up the road, alone."

Gypsy Rose straightened up in her chair. "Most businesses don't want to hire an eleven-year-old with braces and flat feet. I hitchhiked across the coast for a couple of years, eventually settling down and selling seashell jewelry. Of course, tragedy struck again when I found out I was one of only three people in the world who was allergic to seashells."

Jessica made duck lips and shook her head, "The Lord works in mysterious ways. Somehow you found your way back to Cabot Cove and planned your revenge. Eventually getting a job at Kips Seafood and catching the one eye of Clive."

"Poor Clive, I wonder if he ever got that other eye back from that Maine king crap?" Mort asked as his deputy held in his laughter.

Jessica gave them a look and smiled sweetly. She hated to be interrupted. "You got close to him and became like a daughter to the fatherless man. Asking him for advice and patting his ego. When he got comfortable with you, he began confessing his sins over the years and when you found out the extent of what he did to your family, you lost it and told him who you were. Clive laughed at you and told you for the second time in your life to hit the road."

"So, Mrs. F, did they hit the sheets or not?"

Jessica ignored the question. "That's when you struck him and pushed him into the lobster tank and poor Clive, heavy as a Maine rock and not a swimmer, drowned."

Gypsy Rose stuttered and looked confused. She did remember confronting Clive but couldn't remember what happened after that. Maybe she did kill Clive?

Jessica made her rather large eyes wider, "It's okay, dear. We know it was a mistake and not premeditated. He stole your house and shot your dog—"

"—He shot my dog?"

"Yes, and if my information is correct, he laughed about it.

Mort raised his eyebrows and always admired how Jessica seemed to pull information out of thin air.

"Poor Sparky."

"You blacked out, and in a rage, killed him. It wasn't your best moment but it's okay."

Mort put on a smile. He was also impressed by how Jessica Fletcher could ease a suspect into confessing their crimes.

"I was mad at Clive for ruining my life. When he laughed and dismissed me, I realized nobody likes being a fisherman's prostitute."

Jessica blushed when hearing the dirty word, though if she was honest, it did describe the girl.

Gypsy Rose blew her nose. "I just remember seeing black and white—you know, like those cookies—and I had this feeling like I was on fire." She broke down crying. "I did kill him!"

Jessica rubbed Gypsy Rose's cheek and the gesture calmed the frightened woman. "When you get out of the slammer in 10-15 years, I'll bake you some blueberry scones, I know how much you love my blueberry scones."

Mort rather preferred Jessica's double fudge brownies.

Jessica stood her bike up and hopped on, taking one last look at the police station before she rode off. The ride through town would burn off those two prune Danish she mooched from the police station. In her experience, the police always had the best snacks around.

It was a beautiful day in Cabot Cove, and she had many things to do. As Jessica farted and waved at various neighbors on her way home, she couldn't help but smirk when thinking how she got away with framing someone for murder again.

She knew some of her ardent and older fans would probably blush till Tuesday if they knew the real J.B Fletcher but here are the facts; most of her victims were monsters and the person she'd get convicted wouldn't be any better.

Gypsy Rose had been on her death list—right next to her shopping list—darn, I never did get those lemons—Gypsy had been on the list since Jessica caught her stealing chocolate bars from Blind Brenda, who owns Cabot Cove's oldest newspaper and candy store on Main street. Truth be known, old Brenda should have sold the place since half the chocolate she sold was expired but stealing from her was a horrible thing.

Gypsy Rose was stealing so much chocolate, locals pretended to buy invisible bars of candy. The town was worried Blind Brenda— who had been eating her feelings and put on a lot of weight—would become upset if she knew of the theft and try to commit suicide by throwing herself off the Cabot Cove lighthouse again. Lucky for her, that time, Old Man Cooper was fishing by the lighthouse and Blind Brenda landed safely on his boat after jumping. Old Man Cooper wasn't so lucky and was buried a week later in a very thin coffin.

It was her moral obligation to rid the earth of bad people. Jessica bit her lip when thinking murder had started tickling her cookies.

"Good afternoon, Pete."

"Hello, Jessica. Beauty of a day, huh? I heard Gypsy Rose has confessed to the murder."

Jessica thought the internet had nothing on Cabot Cove's gossip mill.

"Now, Pete, you know I don't talk about Mort's cases."

"Why not, Jess, it's usually you who solves them!"

Jessica managed a polite smile and waved him off as she peddled away. As a former English teacher, she always took pride in being smarter than most people, though she didn't like to brag or show off like a lot of women these days.

Before she could even stop her bike, a fancy red car with its roof open tailed her so closely her bike crashed into a tree. The last thing Jessica remembered was the driver, a bleached-to-death blonde talking on her phone and not watching the road.

Moments later, Jessica awoke, coughing. The bleached blonde had stuck a bottle of very expensive and strong perfume to her nose to wake her.

"Oh, God. I killed a senior citizen!"

Jessica pushed the perfume from her face and sat up. She was groggy but being called a senior citizen did more to wake her up than anything.

After a few minutes, the strange woman helped her up. Jessica was happy to see that the only thing bruised was her ego.

"You should be taking a bus at your age. The roads are for the young."

Jessica looked into the deep lines on the woman's face and half-smiled. "Here, in Cabot Cove, we drive slowly so we don't hit the old folk."

"Oh, is that where I am? Good, Lord. I better get going. I'm on my way to a wedding. So sorry for the bump."

Dazed, Jessica took a moment to get her groceries and bike back on the road, the blonde woman applied another layer of make-up. "Now, remember, dear. Take the bus next time, it's air-conditioned and safe for a woman of your advanced years."

As the woman sped off, dust blew in Jessica's face, and she coughed. The woman's frizzy blonde hair blew around from her open car rooftop. Jessica dumped her groceries and put her peddle to the metal and followed her on her bike, picking up a crowbar that sat by the side of the road along the way.

The blonde blasted her music and was on the phone again. When they got to a deserted part of the road, Jessica sped up on her bike and whacked the blonde in the head, sending her right over the cliff and into Cabot Cove bay.

***

As Jessica paused at her house backdoor, she tried to juggle a new bag of groceries, Mara's famous to-go coffee and finding her house keys. She was surprised to find her backdoor open. Creeping inside she was met with the portly backside of one Dr. Seth Hazlitt, Cabot Cove's crusty white-haired doctor, and her good friend.

Seth was peeking in the cookie jar as usual with crumbs on his shirt. She bit her tongue and was most pleased she had laced her famous brownies with Exlaxx. If she couldn't help her friends diet, she sure could help him lose some water weight in the bathroom.

"Seth! I hope you only had one."

"Jessica Fletcher. I'll have you know I was just counting your brownies for you—kind of taking inventory."

Jessica placed her paper bag on the counter and smirked at her old friend. When her dear husband, Frank Fletcher, died, many from town gave their support but it was Dr. Seth Hazlitt, who kept her mind off her pain with a murder case. After solving the murder for Sheriff Tupper, who was the sheriff before Mort Metzger. She found herself thirsty for the next mystery. When none appeared, Jessica soon found her first victim and a whole new career as a novelist. And a serial killer.

"I noticed suitcases by the door. Where are you off to now?"

"Oh, Seth, I've told you several times where I'm going?"

"A'yu, and you can tell me one more time, woman."

"My good friend, Sweetie, is getting married for the first time at forty-one-years old. I'm so happy for her; the poor thing has longed for so many years to get a ring, but no man ever offered.

"Ah, maybe Sweetie isn't so sweet."

"Oh, Seth! She's getting married on a cruise ship."

"Some fancy, long, drawn-out affair, I assume?"

"I'm afraid so. It seems people are stuck on these destination weddings nowadays. It's a cruise to the Greek Islands and we leave from Rome. I shouldn't complain, my family has all but stopped inviting me to events. I guess they think wherever I go, a dead body or two follows."

They both laughed but secretly, Seth, thought her family was on to something. "Sweetie is the woman from your building in New York? The one who came into a load of money recently?"

"Well, when her father got killed by a ten-gallon container of mozzarella that fell out of

Kay's pizza plane, she lost her dear dad but became a rich woman thanks to a six-million-dollar settlement and a year's supply of garlic knots."

"Garlic knots? Isn't she getting married pretty quickly?"

"Yes, just a year after her father's death. Seth, I have to admit, I'm worried about her. I hope this guy isn't marrying her for her money and garlic knots. When I see Sweetie online, she is buying wildly and showing off. The French call it nouveau riche."

"Jess, you can't blame her for going a little wild. From what you told me, she pretty much stayed home every night and read romance novels before her father's death."

Jessica thought bitterly how Sweetie never read any of her books. "Yes, her father was always sickly, and she cared for him. I can't help but be worried for her. Many have killed for less."

Seth took another brownie and stuck it into his mouth quickly. He didn't realize that he had a brown ring around his mouth. "Stop being a mystery writer for once and relax. I'm sure everything will go fine, and your friend Sweetie will have a wedding she'll never forget."

"I'm counting on it." The gleam in her eye was sharp. "What's a matter, Seth. You look like you don't feel well."

"Oh, I better get going. Oh! maybe I'll just use your bathroom first. Seth's body moved quickly out of the room. In all of her years on earth, she'd never seen a man move so fast.

Jessica waited a moment before she burst out laughing. It was a mean thing to do to her friend, but she knew it was for his own good and maybe it would teach him a lesson.

A bewildered Seth came back into the kitchen ten minutes later, staggering, "Oh, that was something, I better get to work—oh, wait—oh!" Seth beat it back upstairs to the guest bathroom.

Jessica threw her head back in laughter. She hadn't laughed this hard since her last murder.

***

As Jessica fixed her eye make-up in the back of a car service on the way to the airport, she picked up her buzzing phone.

"Oh, Mort. Hi, I'm just on my way to the airport—"

"—Jessica, I'm sorry to bother you, but we found a crashed car and a body on the side of the road, out on Dykeman."

"Oh, my stars, how awful."

"Yeah, it always is, anyway, I was wondering if you could maybe drop by. I've come to learn a feminine touch can be helpful in a homicide."

"How flattering you are, and as you know, I love a good mystery but I'm sorry, Mort, you're going to have to do this one on your own, my friend needs me more."

With a laugh, Jessica ended the call and hoped she covered all her tracks after leaving the nasty blonde. She must remember to find out the woman's name from Mort, her family deserves a nice muffin basket.

Chapter Two

Captain Gist stood on the upper deck and rubbed his neatly trimmed grey beard. He smirked watching the cascade of rich guests boarding his ship. They brought with them name-brand labels, doctor enhanced faces and plenty of ideas of what they could complain about. Sometimes, he wondered if he should just walk away and maybe buy a farm somewhere.

He'd rather French kiss a lizard than do that.

Life on the sea could be tough and that was just Mother Nature's fault. The life that he created aboard Seamen's Delight was his real problem and for the most part his fault. It was hard being so good-looking and a shame to waste it on one person. If the good Lord wanted him to stay faithful; he would have never given him such beautiful hair and a smile that could light a whale's butthole.

"Hello, my captain. Doesn't look like a full ship this trip, huh?"

Cruise director, Jula, was half Brazilian, half Japanese and a total knockout, though many thought her frosty blue contacts made her look like a space alien.

Captain Gist rubbed his beard, "Yes. We haven't been fully booked for a year now, but we must be positive things will pick up."

"I know, just because a few passengers died after eating some expired butter—the ones that survived got 50% off their next cruise, what more do they want?" Jula said with a yawn.

"Things are changing on the high seas. I'm thinking it might be time to hang up the white suit and return to dry land."

"You always say you're ready for retirement, but the sea is in your blood and unfortunately on your head—clarifying shampoo will take that yellow waxy build-up from your hair after two washes."

"Forget about my hair. A passenger complained about you. Said you were rude with her for stuffing wings in her purse."

Jula flared her nose and clutched her fists, "She's a dirty liar. I just told her to bring her suitcase next time, her pocketbook couldn't fit all the stuff she stole from the buffet."

"Listen, we all know most of our passengers are either old as rocks or fat as hogs, but we can't insult them. I have too many things going on to worry about this now and I'm sick of telling you to be friendlier to the passengers—that's your job—to bullshit people."

Jula wet her lips, "I'm sorry."

"You're sorry? I'm sick of sorry. Get it together or find another job. I could train a monkey to do your job and only have to give it bananas."

"Bananas? How could you be so rude to the woman who irons your socks and gives you pedicures?"

"Keep your vodka hole shut about that."

"I think you just need a little loving to perk you up. Should I meet you in the boiler room around 3, hiding in the dirty laundry cart like usual?

Captain Gist winched and thought he had sunk to a new low.

He could usually do better than a cruise director.

She touched his arm and he pulled away as if she had lice.

"Don't worry, I'm not about to tell your dear wife or even tell your boyfriend!"

The look on his face made Jula laugh and gave her the power she'd been thirsting for all her life. As a young girl, she had been poor and unloved. Now she made it her life's ambition to make everyone suffer for it.

"So, I guess I can count on seeing you later."

"I don't know what you're talking about, boyfriend? That's sick. I'm all man, baby. I thought you'd know that better than most."

"What's sick is a married man who has such a large ego that he can't stop gorging on every pretty thing in his playpen. Men, women or tree trunks, it doesn't matter to you as long as you do your dirty deed." Jula tried to spit on the ground in anger, but it landed on her uniform and not the floor. She tried not to look embarrassed, but her cheeks told the truth.

He raised a hand to strike her but stopped when he realized his pint-sized second in command was approaching them.

"Good morning, Captain, hello Jula. What a beautiful day this is. God is giving us all of his best today," Fabian announced. "And I like it."

"I'll talk to you later about that matter." Captain Gist said.

"I'm done talking," Jula left in a huff. "The time now is for action."

"Well, well. It seems like she's on her period again" Fabian laughed and put his hands on his hips after giving Captain Gist some papers.

"That's not nice to say about one of your co-workers, though a pretty accurate description."

Fabian winked at the captain and scurried off when someone called from below. A moment later, a large wind seemed to carry a woman dressed in flowing lavender silks up the stairs. With a devilish smile, she bit her lip and sashayed her way over to the captain. Fabian stopped on the stairs to give her a death stare. She ignored him.

"Darling... dearest... surprise!"

Indeed, it was. His wife didn't usually come on his voyages anymore.

Captain Gist reluctantly kissed his wife's painted cheek. "I'm shocked to see you."

"I bet; I thought it was high time we had a good old fashion talk."

He started to sweat and found himself stuttering. When an employee approached them with some questions, she gave him a quick wave of her hand and was off, leaving the fragrance of lavender behind.

"Talk to you later—stud of the sea. I'll be making myself comfortable in the adjoining room next to yours as usual."

Jessica Fletcher stepped out of the darkness and held in a sneeze as Velma walked past. She might just kill her for the crime of wearing too much perfume. What was with some women; thinking they had to smell like a perfume salesperson at Macy's?

Over the years, Jessica found she could learn her best information by hiding in shadows, behind garbage cans, potted palms and, even fat people sometimes. She found gambling rather vulgar, but if she was a betting gal, she'd place all of her money that this cruise was going to be one juicy killing spree... luckily, she packed a knife and fork.

Jessica went down a couple of stairs and paused. The view of the ship from above was breathtaking and it made her think of her husband, Frank. The first time she ever went on a cruise, it was with him.

After letting out a sigh, she took in the scenery as the wind styled her hair like a blind hairdresser. From her view, she could see how huge the boat was. Two large pools sat in the middle like kissing cousins and a winding staircase went up to a private gold hot tub surrounded by tropical plants.

Her smile turned sour when she saw a young woman's head disappearing beneath a man's legs in the hot tub and she blinked her large eyes several times until she realized it was what she thought. Jessica gripped the railing as her heart raced. Sex, in her opinion, was overrated. She'd rather have a king-sized Snickers candy bar and a good cup of tea.

A flag on a long wooden pole that was within reach was her first thought to use on the class-less couple.

She pulled the flag out of the stand and stared at the sharp end. This would pierce the two horn-dogs quickly. Jessica put it back when thinking about how two deaths would probably end the cruise right away this early on. She would wait until they got further out to sea and besides, she had bigger pickles to fry as victims went.

"What do you do for a living?" asked a teenage girl with too much make-up and a sparkly outfit.

Jessica put on a smile and thought it was best to play nice. "I'm an author."

"Only losers read books."

Jessica bit her tongue and thought the rude, young girl was even younger than she appeared to be. She overheard the girl introduce herself as Twinkles Monroe to some other passengers and even danced for them. The girl did a dance that was a combination of ballet, salsa and twerking. The couple Twinkles danced—or whatever it was—for must have not been important enough as well because the girl said something rude to the couple and moved on.

Hopefully, she wouldn't run into the pint-sized pea-brain again.

The large gothic name of the ship stared at her like a disapproving gym teacher. Jessica descended the stairs and stopped again to get another look at the gold, gothic sign. Seamen's Delight was a pretty crude name for a ship if anybody asked her and it was a shame they didn't. If she didn't spring into action, this cruise would soon become one big orgy and that was something a lady of her years and bad back declined to take part in.

Soon a murder would happen, and all the attention would be on her. Now she was off for a glass of mint tea. It helped her to think about how she was going to kill somebody.

In the shadows, a man had been watching Jessica Fletcher. He threw down his cigarette and walked away, stopping to ogle two bikini beauties strolling by. They ignored him and it made him mad. Why were beautiful girls so stuck up?

His thoughts went to the older woman manhandling the flag. He didn't trust women with big eyes, they were always trouble and this old broad had the biggest eyeballs he'd ever seen.

Either, this woman was having some sort of fit or she was trouble. If he had to guess; she looked like the typical kleptomaniac. She probably had her eyeballs on somebody's diamond necklace or if she couldn't get her paws on that, he'd seen people with that condition grab an old pair of tennis shoes and run, anything for the thrill of thievery.

He would watch her closely and when the old gal poached something, he would bring her to his office and handcuff her to a chair. Some would say his methods were cruel, but the truth was he'd have plenty of prune strudel for the old bat; she sure wouldn't get her fiber in these foreign prisons when they docked.

Mr. McCree stared at another pretty girl with red hair and wondered if the rug matched the drapes. He wiped the smile off his face when he saw Captain Gist.

"Wasting time as usual Mr. McCree?" Captain Gist asked with disdain.

"Good morning, Sir."

"I want to see you with your clothes unwrinkled and your shoes shiny enough to see my handsome face. This is not some cheap cruise where you can crawl out of bed and go to work with Oreo crumbs on your chin."

Mr. McCree brushed his chin with his left hand, "I try but I forget, Sir."

"I've told you before, so remember this— either shape up or ship out, now get out of my face—you turd."

Mr. McCree walked and cursed under his breath until Captain Gist was out of sight. He tried in vain to do things right for his boss, but nothing was ever good enough. He was so angry now he was shaking. Some cardio at the ship's gym would cool him down; if he didn't control his anger, he would go and kill the bastard.

***

Jessica sat with her friend and soon to be bride, Sweetie.

"Oh, Jess, I'm so happy you made it. What I've always admired about you is your willingness to appear at social events stag."

"Thank you, Sweetie. After Frank died, I couldn't think about another man, at least not in that way… Now, enough about me. Where is your fiancé?"

"Oh, wait until you meet him! He is the best man I've ever met."

Jessica's smile stayed tight, and they shared some wedding talk. It was cruel to think but she couldn't believe someone would marry her. She had affection for Sweetie but the simple truth was; the girl had been beaten with the ugly stick at birth.

Jessica laughed when she thought of what her mother used to say about unattractive children. "God took the day off when that baby was born and left it up to his simple-minded assistant."

As Sweetie went on about her wedding, Jessica tried not to doze off. Soon, she was wide-eyed and staring at the captain's wife, Velma, as she slinked across the deck and ordered a drink at the bar, openly flirting with the bartender.

Jessica couldn't believe her ill manners but was intrigued by her messy behavior. She could also see how thin Velma was because of her lavender backless dress and plunging neckline that told the world she didn't—but should—wear a bra.

A gaggle of women joined Jessica and Sweetie at their outdoor table. One overly excited redhead stuck a vail on Sweetie and another ordered mimosa's—This wasn't Jessica's favorite drink; tepid orange juice and cheap champagne—but she sipped the orange gruel like a pro and fake laughed her way through it.

By the time Velma was on her fourth cocktail and bored with flirting with every male and potted plant in sight, she turned her attention to the bridal party.

"You're making a mistake, honey," Velma said with a burp. The women at the table cried out with gasps of sighs and outrage. Jessica grabbed her pearl necklace in shock but secretly was hoping for a little action.

Sweetie tried to smile but wasn't ready to give up the attention she was receiving. "Do I know you, dearie?"

Velma blinked her heavily lavender and black colored eyelashes, "No. but I know you. You think you're in love—and you might even be but as soon as the ring goes on your finger, he'll be out the door and onto the nearest tramp."

Jessica didn't like Velma's direct gaze when she said the word 'tramp' but pretended not to notice and gave a reassuring tap on Sweetie's knee. A few women at the table seemed like they would weep if the captain's intoxicated wife went any further.

Sweetie drank the rest of her mimosa. "My Rob is the kindest, sweetest man I've ever known. I'm sorry if you've had some hard luck with love but I can't wait to be Mrs. Sweetie Pie."

"Your man's last name is Pie?" A shocked girl at the table with pointy teeth asked.

"P.Y.E. Pye, not pie."

Jessica concentrated hard not to roll her large eyes and noticed all of the other women at the table looked equally stunned. Sweetie Pye? The woman will be a walking joke to anyone who gets a look at her ID or credit card.

Velma looked like she was either going to laugh or throw-up. Jessica hoped it wasn't the first one, she just bought her dress, and it was an original Margery Rhoades. The designer's clothes were highly sought after because she got herself murdered at a fashionable gym in New York. Dead fashion designers always made people want to own their clothes. The bold print on the dress brought out her eyes or at least she thought so.

Fabian rushed over with another member of the crew and they both stood at opposite ends of the lavender clad beauty who took turns weaving right and left.

"Please, Miss Velma. It's time for bed." Fabian said, grabbing her left arm. The attendant took her right arm and they both quickly tried to steer her towards the door, but she dug her four-inch heels into the floor like they were spikes and both men twisted their necks with a bonus of whiplash.

"Back off, you little gay shrimp! And you too, you red-faced Irish leprechaun from hell. Help me! They are trying to rape me!" Velma screamed, staring at Sweetie in such a way, Jessica got chills.

This got the attention of the room, and everyone looked shell-shocked. A few well-meaning men took their napkins off their laps to help but were quickly distracted by the crew members that poured in like an army, people stood back in wonder. Only one elderly man with a dead battery in his hearing aid and poor eyesight kept eating his spaghetti and meatballs, oblivious to the melee.

Two crewmen held her as the ship's doctor attended to Fabian and the Irish man, eventually putting neck braces on both of them. Besides the pain in their necks, both men felt embarrassed about what Velma had said about them. Fabian tried to stand up straight, hoping to appear taller. The Irish lad was at a loss on how to appear less Irish looking.

Jessica cleaned her teeth with a toothpick politely under a napkin and thought she should put Velma out of her misery. She opened her ears and could make out that the crew had mixed opinions on how to take care of the captain's crazy spouse. Velma was their boss's wife but still assaulted two fellow officers, even if they were a fruit and an Irishman.

"Calm down Mrs. Gist or we'll have to cuff you. Let's take you to your husband." An officer with too much hair gel said. "He'll want to deal with this."

"No, put her in the brig and lock the door. Oh, oh, my beautiful swan-like neck is ruined!" Fabian barked, looking like he would faint at any moment.

"Unhand me, you fiends!" Velma still stared at Sweetie with malice, "I want to speak to her!"

Sweetie looked away as her bridal party gave her positive reassurances. The woman was certified Loony Toons and desperate to ruin Sweetie's happiness.

More crew from Seamen's Delight entered and they were able to pull Velma towards the door as a good-looking man with golden-brown hair that matched his eye color walked into all the confusion.

Sweetie squeezed Jessica's hand and squealed with delight, "That's him, the love of my life, the match to my sweaty gym socks, the icing to my carrot cake—"

"—I get the picture, dear," Jessica said with a genuine smile.

"Rob! Beloved, oh, yoo-hoo! we're over here."

Rob was more interested in Velma. "Get your filthy paws off my mother!"

"Mother? Why didn't he tell me his mother was on this ship?" Sweetie fainted head first into her chocolate mousse, splashing Jessica's dress. Jessica let out a quiet but deadly smelling fart. This was going to be one interesting voyage.

Chapter Three

After spending more than two hours in the ship's jail, Velma was marched into the bridge. Captain Gist handed over the steering wheel to a crew member and went over to Velma.

"What have you gotten yourself into now?"

Velma ignored his question and slapped him in the face, "How dare you not tell me my son was on board and how dare you not tell me you repainted this room!"

A crew member pulled her back and waved his hands in front of her face, "Don't light a match, her breath is lethal—yikes!"

"Unhand my wife, officer. Velma, listen to me. I didn't know you were coming aboard, let alone your son. I did some checking when you were sleeping it off in our jail; why don't you ask Rob why he didn't tell you he was going to be getting married on this ship? Instead of making a fool of yourself."

This seemed to shock Velma and sober her up. She stared around the room at all the eyes and then back to the red-cheek of her husband.

"You're all trying to drive me crazy! I'm not crazy!"

"Officer, can you take my wife to her cabin and bring her a big pot of coffee?"

"Yes, sir."

Jessica walked into the bridge. The EMPLOYEES ONLY sign was invisible to her. "Oh, excuse me. Oh, my, you poor dear. Can I be of any help?"

"Mind your own business—you old banana." Velma spat.

Jessica tried not to laugh or seem pissed. Two emotions she felt at the moment. Maybe she'd leave a banana peel for Velma, and she could fall off the deck and become shark food.

"Velma! Don't be so rude," Captain Gist said.

"This lovely lady was just trying to help."

"Don't worry, I see the poor woman is distressed and in need of some rest." And a good make-up artist.

"Wait a minute, I know you. You were on TV last month!" Velma said, trying to free her hands from the crewmen that were trying to steer her towards the door.

Jessica glowed with false modesty as everyone stared at her.

"A celebrity on board Seamen's Delight, what a delight!" Captain Gist said, making his crew fake laugh and introducing himself with a sweaty handshake.

"Jessica Fletcher, nice to meet you, captain—"

"That's not your name!" said Velma as the captain tried to ignore his wife and introduce himself.

"Well, I do write under J.B Fletcher."

"No, that's not the name I saw you use. You were on Judge Judy last month; you stole somebody's monkey and wouldn't give him back."

"I think you are mistaken, dear."

"Where's that monkey!" Velma demanded and Jessica looked to the captain for help.

The crew pulled Velma out of the bridge and that gave Jessica a good view of the room that controlled the ship.

"I'm sorry Miss. Fletcher—"

In the distance, you could vaguely here Velma screaming. "Check her room! She's got that monkey!"

"That's Mrs. Fletcher, Captain Gist, though my husband has been dead for some years."

"Oh, well, then. I'll alert the single men. A beautiful mature gal is on board and looking for action."

Jessica's mouth opened in shock, but she quickly hid her feelings. "You flatter me." She wasn't flattered as the captain's eyes looked her over like a menu. The man seemed perpetually hungry.

The captain squeezed her shoulders, and it made her wince. "Please, be my guest tonight at the captain's table. Hopefully, a wonderful dinner and the most glittering company can make up for a rather bad situation. My wife, when she drinks…"

Jessica waited for him to go on. When he didn't, she accepted his invitation and hoped the wife would be sleeping it off and not making an appearance at dinner. It would also be a perfect time to sneak down to her room and kill her. If anyone deserved to die it was her. Sweetie would be accused because of the scene Velma made at her bridal party. Jessica would sweep in and find the real killer, probably the grabby husband.

As Jessica left the bridge, her shoulders cringed when overhearing Captain Gist berate his staff.

"Hey, flat ass! Keep the wheel steady… Sheila, wake up! Or has your face always looked like that?"

Jessica hated bed language and was beginning to think Captain Gist was the one who should be put out of his misery.

Chapter Four

Fabian wined in dramatic pain as the ship's doctor left his cabin with his medical bag. He sprayed himself with perfume and put on large sunglasses. He looked more like a Hollywood star after plastic surgery then a man who just suffered whiplash.

Captain Gist entered and looked down on Fabian and held a smile in. If he wasn't careful, he'd have a lawsuit on his hands with this one. He was already informed that an Irish crew member was threatening to sue for discrimination.

"Now, there. You're going to be just like new in three or four months."

Fabian pulled his sunglasses to his nose and raised them again. "Are you kidding? I'll have to wear this neck brace the whole time and, in this sunny weather, I'll have a white ring around my neck. This just won't do."

"I could lay you off and you could get off the ship at the next port."

Fabian pouted and wondered what he would do. The only thing he had to go back home to was a goldfish, Herman, and odds were, he was floating on top of the water in his tank after all this time.

"I just don't know what to do. I feel like a caged, beautiful bird if I have to stay in this room until the next port."

"I think you should get your pitiful self dressed and in uniform and back to work like a man. All you need is some energy."

When Captain Gist turned off the lights, Fabian wiggled with delight until his neck hurt too much."

"Oh captain, full steam ahead!"

Ten minutes later as Captain Gist snuck out of Fabian's room, fixing his belt, Jula stepped out of the shadows with one single tear flowing down her face.

As her nostrils flared, Jula went over to the railing of the ship and lost her cookies. In her anger, she thought she was throwing up into the water. Two angry sunbathers yelled up at her. Later, she would comp them two free bottles of water to make up for the mess, right now she was paralyzed to move. The rage she felt for Captain Gist was explosive.

"I'll show him to break my heart in pieces, I'll show them all!"

As Jessica took a run around the ship in a pink jumpsuit, she bumped into a portly fellow with an apple-shaped head and frizzy, red hair.

"You are the mystery writer, J.B Fletcher, I assume?"

"Why, yes, but call me Jessica and you are?"

The odd-looking man introduced himself as Damon McCree, chief security officer.

"Oh, do you always introduce yourself personally to all the guests?"

"Only the ones I see hiding in dark parts of the ship on camera."

Jessica threw her scarf around her neck and followed his gaze to the device focused on them hanging from the wall. "For these prices, I'll go anywhere on this ship I want."

"My dear, I didn't mean to offend you."

"I'm not offended, just taken aback."

After he tipped his hat to her, Jessica nodded and walked quickly around the corner with her head up until Mr. McCree was out of sight. She'd have to watch this guy; he might be smarter than he looks. She also had a feeling he might be up to something.

***

Jessica took a stroll around the ship before dinner and ran into cruise director Jula on deck.

"Mrs. Fletcher, don't you look stunning. You could be Jennifer Lopez's twin."

Jessica's distaste for the comment showed and she forced a cough. "Thank you, but I think you're stretching the truth a bit."

"Ha! Well, you know what I mean. How is your trip so far?"

"Marvelous. The weather is great and my rooms a dream. How are you?"

Fear showed through her odd-looking blue contacts. "I'm okay—Just busy as usual working on all the events for the cruise. Do you believe in astrology, Mrs. Fletcher?"

"I can't say I follow it but if I see my horoscope, I usually read it. Why do you ask?"

"I'm a Leo and my horoscope today said that I should be aware of the color lavender."

Jessica's mind flashed to the captain's wife, Velma. "I don't think you should take those things too seriously. They're just for fun."

"There is something in the air tonight, I can feel it."

Jessica's eyes bugged out and felt her fists tightening. She calmly wet her lips, "Is it murder?"

"No, I think it's fish. Don't you just hate when people at work heat fish in the microwave? There should be a law against that."

Jessica couldn't hide her confusion and rolled her eyes. Jula didn't notice, she was too busy digging in the fancy name-brand designer purse around her waist. Fanny-pack is what they used to call it but nowadays who knew? Jessica tapped her foot as Jula applied glittery lip gloss as if possessed. She should just kill her for being annoying.

When she was ready to speak, Jessica's stomach felt woozy looking at Jula's mouth. Why women thought it was attractive to look as if you covered your lips in lard and dipped them in glitter was beyond her comprehension.

"Did anyone tell you about the costume ball in two nights?

Jessica couldn't imagine why a cruise would have this kind of event. Dressing up could be fun but in this unbearable heat on a boat? "How amazing but I'm afraid I didn't pack a costume with my suntan oil."

"Jula's eyes flared, and Jessica realized the costume ball was something in which Jula had a hand in. This seemed to be the only thing the cruise director was interested in besides her married lover, Captain Gist.

"We have a full supply of outfits in every shape and size, Mrs. Fletcher if you're worried you won't fit into anything."

Jessica pretended like she didn't get the casual dig and thought she'd do some digging herself with a very large shovel. "Will the Captain be at the costume party? He's such a marvelous man, you must be thrilled beyond belief to get to work for him every cruise."

"Captain Gist is a pig, a heathen, a scoundrel and has no place running a ship of this size!"

"Oh, I'm so sorry dear. You sound hurt."

"I don't know what you're talking about. You must have had too many free mimosas for lunch today."

Jessica set her sad puppy eyes on the angry woman and Jula melted.

"I'm just hurt… broken like a beautiful china cup left on the highway after a dog peed on it."

"There's always glue." Jessica hoped Jula didn't consider herself a poet.

"Oh, Mrs. Fletcher, I'm sick of being used by men."

"Maybe forget men for a while and get a cat."

"I had one, but he ran away. Everybody runs from me, oh, hell. I'll make them all pay!"

Jula looked like the kind of woman who lifted various parts of her body at a young age. It took a moment for Jessica to understand, Jula's real scars were invisible to the eye but very deep."

**

The constant knocking on Velma's bedroom door was driving her crazy. Even a thrown lamp did nothing to stop the noise. She got out of bed, lit a cigarette, kicked the broken lamp to the side and opened the door.

"What in tarnation is your problem?"

Rob took her into his arms, and she reluctantly hugged him, breaking into tears. "Oh, Rob! How could you not have told me about your wedding?"

"I wanted to surprise you."

"A puppy would've been better."

After pouring her a glass of water, they sat down. "I didn't tell you because I knew you wouldn't approve."

Velma rubbed her head, "I could have learned to, Oh, Rob, don't you see? My marriage is crumbling, and my only son is marrying a woman older than dirt."

"We're only eleven years apart in age."

"That's her story, you should check her passport."

Rob stood up and straitened his bow tie. "See, this is why I didn't tell you about Sweetie. You know mother, maybe this is why everyone is mad at your—your ill-temper and bad habit of never brushing your teeth."

When her son left, Velma threw herself on the bed sobbing and kicking her feet in the air. She did smell onions on her breath but didn't care and thought a son should respect his mother, no matter what she did or had for lunch. She didn't blame herself for her son's cruel words. It was this woman he was marrying; she was the problem and turned Rob against her.

Her son was an angel until he met that New York woman with a stupid name. When he served time in jail, they even let him out for good behavior. He was a wonderful son until he met that woman.

Jessica sat at the captain's table having a glass of white wine and making small talk. When Captain Gist asked her to dance, she wanted to refuse because her foot was aching after kicking the side of the bed this morning. She limped to the dance floor; this was a perfect opportunity to get more information about Velma from him. If she was going to kill one of them, it was better to know which strawberry in the bunch was mostly rotten.

The ballroom was a large space with round windows surrounding half the room. The sea was a rowdy vision of whites and blues as they danced the Tango. When Captain Gist dipped her, Jessica heard her back crack. She couldn't help noticing the glass ceiling and how fluffy and close the clouds seemed as if she could reach up and touch them.

"I promise to be gentle, my sweet lady— well, as long as we're standing that is." He licked her ear like a dog, a dog that hadn't been spayed yet.

Jessica felt her grilled cheese wanting to come up, "You are a very charming man, Captain Gist. How long have you been working on boats?"

"I know... I was born on a ship, dear lady. My mother took a cruise and some rough weather decided I was to be born a month early. I came into the world smelling the salty air and this is how I will leave it."

"Oh, my, your poor mother!"

The soft, romantic music was interrupted by blasting noise. Both Jessica and Captain Gist covered their ears in pain but still moved their feet in unison. The over fifty generation soon learned it was rap music being played and most of the people on the dance floor gave up trying to groove to the strong beats and aggressive voices and just stood around confused.

Jessica followed Captain Gist's eyes up to the see-through box of the deejay booth. Inside was Sweetie's soon-to-be husband, Rob, rocking to the beat with his baseball cap on backwards as a thin man with many arm tattoos pounded on the glass door.

"Oh, ham and eggs, what's going on?" Jessica asked as the music was cut off abruptly.

"Rob, get out of there! Somebody call security! Where is that bumbling fool, Mr. McCree?" Captain Gist yelled up at the deejay booth. Now Jula and the real deejay were trying to get the door open.

Jessica knew who Rob was but found it best to play dumb. "Who is that rude man?"

"I take no pleasure in admitting that man is my stepson and a total waste of space."

As heavy bass beats shot from the speakers, the crowd of seniors on the dance floor parted and out came pint-sized Twinkles Monroe, twirling a glittery baton and doing ballerina poses. She resembled a child dressed up like a hooker, singing along to the music.

"Dem men, dem men, want to do me, oh, them men, try to abuse me, but I say no, I'm no Burger King ho. Oh, oh, no!"

Twinkles Monroe danced, twirled her baton and sang in a circle around Jessica and Captain Gist, making them both dizzy as they watched her. Jessica realized this was the young girl who had told her 'only losers read books' when she first arrived on the ship. She had the urge to stamp on the mini songstress-from-hell with her One-inch pumps but suppressed her anger and covered her mouth in shock.

"Dem men, them men, want to do me, abuse me but I say no, I'm no Burger King ho. Oh, oh, no!"

When the music stopped, Twinkles went on rapping or singing or whatever it was. The lyrics sounded even funnier without the beats, especially since Twinkles and her voice hadn't quite reached maturity. Jessica couldn't help but think of the munchkin's singing in The Wizard of Oz.

"Dem men, them men, want to do me, abuse me but I say no, I'm no Burger King ho. Oh, oh, no!"

Jessica looked up to see Rob being dragged out of the DJ booth. The poor crew had their hands full of wacky passengers.

"Twinkles, come over here at once!" Captain Gist yelled.

Reluctantly, Twinkles soon dropped her mini mic and baton on the floor and stood in front of them with a chip the size of Mount Rushmore on her glittery shoulders.

Captain Gist waved his pointy finger at her, "What is the meaning of this? Have you been doing drugs?"

"My dad—I mean, my manger is launching my music and dancing career."

"Not on the Seamen's Delight."

"My stars, what a beautiful dress." Jessica said, trying to cool down the temperature on the dance floor."

"Thanks, momma—though I doubt they'd have your size."

Jessica's eyes bugged out and she thought of slapping the smirk off the young girl but hid her anger and put on a smile.

"Oh, from the mouth of babes." Jessica pinched the girl's cheeks until the little brat almost sobbed."

"Get you donut paws off me, you bug-eyed fool!"

Upstairs in the captain's quarters, Velma, Rob, Twinkles and Captain Gist argued as Jessica lurked in the background.

"I blame you, Velma, for letting your son and granddaughter run amuck and embarrass me."

"I didn't know they were coming…" Velma sobbed.

Velma did seem generally in shock at her son and granddaughter's actions, but Jessica knew some people had better acting-abilities than the biggest of stars. The facts were; Velma did come aboard to confront her husband, probably over his cheating ways. Maybe she encouraged Rob and Twinkles to come aboard and annoy him. And why hadn't Rob told Sweetie they were going on his stepfather's boat? Rob told her he wanted it to be a surprise.

It was. Surprise! Meet your new wacky family.

Captain Gist took a pill bottle from his dresser and swallowed two pale-yellow pills, "I don't believe you. I work most of the year and all three of you benefit from my money, but this is enough! I want a divorce and want you all off the boat when we dock in the first port." Captain Gist opened the door as they all complained.

"I am here getting married unless you want to throw a happy couple off your boat? I'm sure the internet will just love to hear how Seamen's Delight isn't so delightful." Rob said at the door.

"Fine, you can all stay, but no more drama."

Captain Gist looked towards the crashing waves from his balcony window as Velma ran out sobbing and cursing. Rob and Twinkles followed her out but went the opposite way in a huff, not speaking to Velma.

When they were alone, Captain Gist grabbed Jessica and ripped open her blouse.

"You know you want this, Mrs. Fletcher."

"I should say not! Now, please unhand me."

Jessica pushed him off, but the man was like glue and forced a kiss on her that turned Jessica's face blue. Any kind of sexual intimacy was like cough syrup to her, and she smacked him hard across the cheek.

"Oh, you red hot granny, like it rough, huh?"

"Take a cold shower!"

"Why don't you join me?" Captain Gist tripped over his feet and fell over.

Jessica managed to escape the room and only stopped running when she saw Velma standing alone, looking out at the sea.

"Velma… are you okay?"

"You again? You're like a pimple I can't get rid of."

Jessica wanted to tell her to take a swim in Clearasil but turned away instead. Velma stopped her.

"I'm sorry, I'm just so confused. I need a drink. Booze! Booze! Someone bring me a Jack Daniels on the rocks," Velma grabbed the wall and cried.

"Let's go somewhere and have a nice cup of tea."

"Sounds disgusting, I'd rather have a margarita."

"Haven't you had enough?"

Velma nodded her head and they strolled along the deck in silence. A light breeze from the sea and music from one of the ship's ballrooms could be heard in the distance. If Velma didn't have black and lavender color stains running from her eyes, it would have been a lovely moment.

After some small talk and two empty cups of tea sat in front of them. Jessica asked the question everyone on board wanted to know.

"This ship seems to be bringing you nothing but pain, why did you come?"

Velma cleared her throat and for a moment, Jessica thought she would cry again.

"To confront my husband, of course. I know it might be a shock to you, Jessica, but I think the captain—my husband—is having a dirty affair. To tell you the complete truth. I think he's been doing it on this very ship. I feel like I want to end it all."

Jessica looked in horror, but this kind of thing happened so much she was rather bored with the outrage people have. Losing one's trust in the person you loved was understandably annoying but to throw yourself off a cliff because it was a tad dramatic.

"Please don't do anything to hurt yourself. Life is a precious thing. I'm sorry to hear about your marriage but maybe you can work it out."

Before Velma could answer a piece of paper was shoved in front of Jessica's face. Her knee jerk reaction was to push it away.

Fabian stood smiling with what looked like fried chicken grease on his lips but was probably lip gloss. "I know I'm not supposed to bother the guests, but I'm a big fan. Your books helped me to learn English when I came to this country. I love you more than mixed nuts."

"Oh, my stars, how nice. Where are you from?"

"France."

As Jessica scribbled her name down, she thought it was odd how he didn't say from which part of France he was from, most people were proud of their hometowns. Unless her eyes and ears were going, the man looked and sounded more like he came from a Latin country than France. She had noticed before that Fabian's accent was all over the place. Her writer's mind wondered why he could be lying.

She hoped her so-called biggest fan wasn't a terrorist.

"Could I get you some more tea?"

"Buzz off, fruit fly." Velma said with venom.

The short man seemed to grow ten inches in height, even stretching his neck through his brace. "You know, dear, bitter doesn't wear well on your aging face," Fabian said quietly for only the two women to hear and walked off after bowing to Jessica.

When Fabian left, Jessica decided to say something. "Velma, you were horribly rude to that young man."

"You'd be rude too if you knew your man was jumping in bed with that husband-stealing parasite. With all the cheap women in the world and he turns to a hairy man? Why most women even bother to shave anymore beats me. We should just grow body hair like a beast and maybe our husbands will remain faithful. Oh, the inhumanity, dumped for a dude!"

So, Velma did know.

Jessica's phone said it was after two in the morning. She turned it on silent as she crept into Captain Gist's room. She overheard one of the crew saying that the captain retired early because he wasn't feeling well and never locked his door in case of an emergency.

The captain had fallen asleep with his anchor night light on. She had a lovely room but his was spacious and looked like it was a home. His framed, signed photo of 1970's Spanish singer, actress, and musician, Charo, mostly known for her bad English and catchphrase, 'cuchi-cuchi' made Jessica smile. She quietly read the inscription on the photo.

"Dis ship is better than the Love Boat, kisses, Charo."

The captain was sleeping on his side and she was happy about it. Though she had killed a good share of people. It was better to not look into their eyes. Victims could be so queer sometimes—a few had even woken up in shock when she was stabbing them, the look in their eyes could jolt a gal's confidence.

Murder was hard work.

Jessica raised the hammer with one hand, slowly—darn arthritis! —and thought a nice

cup of tea would be great after killing this
sleazy guy.

When she pulled back the covers, her
hammer dropped, and it landed on her foot.
She held in her pain, hopping on one foot. If
anyone heard her, the jig would be up.

Jessica wasn't clumsy, just in shock. Captain
Gist was already dead.

A steel baton sticking through his back and
out of his chest. The tip of the baton had a
star on it and it was sticking out of his chest.
If there wasn't blood mixed with glitter
everywhere, the scene could almost be cute,
like a father playing dead with his kid.

Jessica sucked in her breath and let out the
air. Somebody murdered Captain Gist before
she did?

How rude.

Jessica knew she had to leave the room but
was too curious not to look around for clues.
The first real clue was the baton, she had seen
it before but couldn't remember where. She
made sure to step around the blood and
peeked under the bed. She pulled out a stack

of magazines and frowned when seeing the titles. A pile of old porno magazines laid there. Jessica made a mental note to wash her hands when getting back to her room.

Captain Gist was the horniest man she had ever met.

She wore black gloves but still wiped her prints off the magazines. These days, they could even tell your hand size, so best to be careful.

Jessica went over to his dresser and went through the dead man's belongings. Captain Gist's clothes, even socks, were lined evenly in each drawer by color and looked as if measured by a ruler for accuracy. Probably was a military man.

After pulling several open and finding nothing of interest, she was surprised to find a drawer full of sex toys and gasped loudly, dropping a rather large one.

A quiet knock came at the door and Jessica covered her mouth, quickly putting the wonky object back into the drawer Would this be her fate? Accused and convicted of a murder she didn't commit.

"Oh, Mr. Boss man, I'm here to ask for a day off—a day off your body!... Open up, lover, I heard you in there."

It was Jula.

Jessica slid into the connecting room when the click of the door opened.

"Darling, I'm so happy that we've made up. Now, let your dumpling come and swim in your beef broth."

Jessica rolled her eyes in the other room. Thank heavens, she was the only writer aboard. Just as Jula screamed, Jessica noticed another door and went through it. It was an enjoining room, maybe for his wife. Luckily, Velma wasn't in the empty bed—where was she?

Jessica slipped out Velma's front door and ran around the deck just as lights from other cabin doors came on, no doubt people waking up after hearing the screams.

Jessica made it to her room just in time as room doors started opening. She quickly took off her clothes and put on her robe. Her hair and makeup stayed in place as if put there by magic.

Just where was the captain's wife at this hour? Had she killed him and made a run for it?

Chapter Five

Damon McCree poked his hands threw the unruly red hair on his head. Not only did he have a murderer aboard Seamen's Delight that killed the captain of the ship, but they also did it without him knowing a thing, if only he hadn't fallen asleep with his usual cup of hot cocoa and Golden Girls reruns, he could have walked around the ship and seen something.

Damn those sassy seniors living in Miami for being so funny.

Even though the murder weapon looked like a child's toy, it was strong enough to pierce the skin.

Fabian stood at the door, fanning his face. His neck brace was on and looked crooked.

"Fabian! Get over here!" Mr. McCree demanded.

"Oh, no, no, I just can't look at a dead body."

"Are you a man or a mouse?"

"squeak... squeak... squeak."

Mr. McCree tried not to laugh, "Get over here now or I'm telling the crew to throw you overboard."

Fabian reluctantly took his time coming over to the body and the kneeling head of security. Mr. McCree stood up and looked around the body for clues. He'd never seen a bed that looked so well used. The headboard alone had several head shapes imprinted in the wood.

When Mr. McCree opened the adjoining door and saw that Velma's bed hadn't been slept in, a light bulb blew up in his head, "A-ha!"

Fabian was in tears as his red eyes finally looked at his boss's body. Mr. McCree would wonder later if the feminine young man was just pretending or actually sad about his boss's death.

76

"Is he dead?" Fabian asked, tears flowing.

"What in blazes do you think? He has a baton with a star on top sticking out of his chest."

"Is that a yes?"

"Silence! Now, I want you to pull yourself together and listen. Offhand, do you know if there are any children aboard the ship?"

"Not that I can recall, why do you ask?"

"This baton looks like something a child would use."

"A child murdered the captain? Oh, Lord, no… I told him not to steal candy from babies but he didn't listen. Oh, the horror. Now some cartoon-loving-baby Charles Manson has done him in."

Mr. McCree looked at Fabian like he was crazy and forced him out of the room, "get that information."

As the crew held off nosy passengers, Mr. McCree searched the room. When he found the porn magazines under the bed, he wondered if they were a clue.

"See anything you like, Mr. McCree?" Jessica Fletcher asked with the most innocent smile. When she saw the magazines, she covered her mouth in horror, "Oh, my stars!"

"How did you get in here?"

A crew member peaked in nervously, "I'm sorry, Sir, she said she had information about the murder."

Mr. McCree scoffed and stood up, trying to conceal the magazine titles from Jessica. "Well, I see you have your nose in this, so, spill the chips and tell me what you think you know."

"I'm not trying to step on your perfectly manicured toes, but as soon as I heard of this horrible tragedy, I knew I had to come here as fast as my sensible shoes could take me."

"Get on with it!"

"Well, his wife Velma told me in confidence that she thought her husband was having an affair."

Mr. McCree wrinkled his nose and slid the magazines back under the bed. "And did she tell you who she suspected?"

"Well, that is to say, she had an idea…"

"Spit it out woman or leave."

Jessica tried not to react to Mr. McCree's nasty attitude because she needed to mislead him with information but then she realized that she didn't know who killed Captain Gist. The wife was the obvious choice but something told her there was more to this then a simple wife scorned.

Jessica took a moment to think. Whoever did it was a real spoilsport for ruining her fun but there was a murderer on board and she was going to do her best to solve who killed Captain, Gist even though he deserved it.

"Velma thought her husband was playing 'guess what's in my pants' with Fabian."

Mr. McCree looked confused until Jessica made a hole with her thumb and index finger on her left hand. On her right hand, she used her index finger to poke the hole. It took Mr. McCree a minute to understand and he turned as red as his hair and couldn't stop coughing until one of the crew members patted him hard on the back.

When he composed himself, Mr. McCree smirked and shook his head, almost pitying the nosy old woman.

"In all my years working as a policeman and as a security officer, I have seen a lot of things that could shock an old stripper, but I'll tell you one thing, Mrs. Fletcher, Captain Gist was all man, a real man's man and loved women like flies love—"

"—Please, no vulgarities. I get your point. I'm just telling you what she thought."

"And you just loved the seedy gossip, something juicy for your next book?"

Jessica pretended to look around the room as if for the first time. "If you say so, Mr. McCree. I'm sure you know better than me."

"You got that right, and you can leave right through the door you came in—"

"—Did you notice Captain Gist's fingernails? They are blue."

Mr. McCree rolled his eyes and hardly looked at the body again until he noticed the swollen fingertips.

"This is crazy, they weren't blue minutes ago."

"Of course, the doctor on board can tell you but I think he was poisoned first and then killed with the baton."

Mr. McCree was thinking the same thing and didn't like anyone telling him his job. "I know my job, Mrs. Fletcher and this isn't my first murder." It was his first murder.

Jessica knew when to leave a situation and was about to turn for the door when she saw the hammer she had been carrying to kill Captain Gist laying on the floor in a shadowed area. If Only Jula hadn't barged in, she could have had a minute to think straight and carry the weapon out. Luckily, there were no prints on it. Mr. McCree or someone would soon find it and wonder why it was on the floor. She had no choice and had to leave it.

This was turning out to be her worst vacation ever.

Mr. McCree sat in his office and stared at the photo behind Jula as she wiped her tears. Why people decorated beach houses and boats with pictures of the sea made no sense. You never saw an apartment building with pictures of street lamps or other apartment buildings, so why live on the sea and have pictures of water?

"Oh, Mr. McCree. I can't believe someone killed our wonderful leader."

Mr. McCree wasn't going to pretend to mourn a man who took pleasure in insulting him, "I heard you fault with him yesterday and he dumped you. Was he wonderful then?"

Jula's strange eyes grew and shrunk, almost like a cartoon, "We had a misunderstanding but had worked things out. I hope you don't think anything sexual was going on between us, I'm a church-going, woman."

Mr. McCree held in his laughter. The couple of years he had known Jula, she was known to jump on more men's laps then a small dog. She had affairs with about ten men on the crew and another twenty or so passengers, mostly married. If she needed to pretend to be religious that was her choice, but it gave her a good motive for murder; kill the married man who betrayed her.

"Jula, what were you doing with Captain Gist at this late hour?"

"That is none of your business." She sobbed again.

"Okay ... As if the whole ship didn't know... did you see anyone or hear anything around his door?"

Jula got up and tried to freshen her face in a small compact mirror. "Oh, it's so hard for me to remember. I just can't believe it."

"Now, listen, girl. This is a shock for all of us, but you pledged solidarity when you joined Seamen's Delight. Our leader may be fish food but it's my duty to find who killed him before this ship docks."

"Why do you care, he couldn't stand you."

Mr. McCree ran his hand threw his frizzy red hair, "That may be so, but murder happened on my watch, I'm not losing my job and pension with this on my record so some psycho killer can get off this boat and get a suntan."

With his last word, he looked at Jula with a hard stare. He wasn't sure if she killed him or maybe even had someone else do it for her. One thing he was sure of, she was dirtying the sheets with Captain Gist, which proved he wasn't queer.

"How long do you think it will take after I interview the crew that I'll get proof about you and the captain? Save me some time, sweet cheeks and spill the cat litter."

Jula said nothing for a few minutes. If she lied to him now, it could come back to hurt her.

"The captain and I have been on and off for two years now. Yesterday, he officially dumped me. I admit to making a scene, but I didn't kill him."

"Just for the record, where were you last night before you came to his room?"

Jula's laugh was quiet, almost like a squeak instead of a chuckle. Was she guilty, scared or just testing his patience? Mr. McCree wasn't sure.

"You can look at the crew schedule, it was my night on the late shift. I was on deck C, attending to the few partiers still up and looking for mischief."

"And were you always on deck C?"

Jula's strange eye color betrayed her. "Of course, why would I be anywhere else?"

Mr. McCree rustled through some papers. "I see by your schedule, that you're supposed to be off work about ten minutes ago. So, do not take me for a fool and tell me why you were at the Captain's cabin this time in the morning?"

Jula cried again, knocking out one of her blue contacts. She finally composed herself after searching in vain for the colored eyewear. "Alright—alright. You want the truth? I'll tell you but hold on to your yellowed tighty-whities… I was hoping to get him to make monkey-love to me again. I thought sex would win him back."

"I thought as much unless that's a cover and you just came to end his life like an old dog."

85

Jula looked at Mr. McCree sharply, "Some people think putting an old dog out of its misery is justifiable."

Outside Mr. McCree's office, Jessica moved away from the round window. She didn't think Jula was a suspect. Now, she wondered if Jula killed him earlier and came back to play at being shocked when finding the body. It made sense; the mistress is always the second suspect after the wife. The thought put a snake in her picnic basket—an old saying of her mother.

Usually, she knew all about the murders because she did the murder, now she was faced with a tricky mystery and had to prove her talents as a real amateur investigator before Mr. McCree or anyone else found the culprit. It would burn her biscuits if someone else solved it before her.

Jessica needed a cup of tea or maybe something stronger. There hasn't been a person yet who could outsmart her. She had to think about everything she knew so far.

First, she would go find Velma. Why was his wife not sleeping in her bed next door? Was she sleeping off a drunken stupor or did she run because she killed Captain Gist?

Hopefully, with all the melee, nobody has told her about her husband yet.

Mr. McCree wiped the sweat off his forehead. Twinkles Monroe was such a spoiled child he wished he could slap the smug look from her face. Every rude remark the brat spat at him, the father apologized, he was fed up.

"Twinkles, where were you this evening between midnight and three?"

"In my bed dreaming of fame and fortune, I'm going to have. Where were you? Pissing in your diaper somewhere?"

"Now, dear, that's enough. I'm sorry Mr. McCree, she didn't have her raisin bagel yet," Rob said.

"I was sleeping, all night. Can I go now?"

"Oh, Twinkles, that's not completely true. Like I said, Mr. McCree, I was in bed all night, but I did get up around one to check on her, and she was gone. I was worried but knew my daughter could take care of herself, she does know karate."

Twinkles rolled her eyes as Mr. McCree watched her, "Oh that's right, I woke up and took a stroll around the deck and helped an old lady back to her room."

Rob beamed, "That's my angel, always helping people."

Mr. McCree wondered if the father was dumb or good at playing it, "And how did your baton get stuck in victim's back?"

Rob winched and Twinkles laughed and pulled out a sparkly baton and pointed the steel tip close to Mr. McCree's face "My baton is right here sucker."

When they left, Mr. McCree wondered if a young girl could kill a man of Captain Gist's size. The thought that the father did it for her seemed like a better idea.

Chapter Six

Jessica caught her breath. She hadn't moved that fast since a safe almost fell on her in the 1980s.

It took Jessica a good ten minutes to find a bunch of rolled-up lavender fabric. On the upper deck, passed out on a beach chair was Velma. At first glance, Jessica thought she was dead but then her snoring put an end to that idea and scattered a few birds as well.

Was there anything worse than a snoring drunk?

Whispering Velma's name softly did nothing to rouse the brick that was Velma.

"Free wine, come one, come all, free wine!"

Velma rolled off the bench to the floor and was on her feet, sporting crossed eyes within a minute.

"Where? Where? What deck is the free wine on?" Velma cried in a voice so deep, Jessica wondered if she was a man.

"Oh, my stars, you poor dear. There you are!" Jessica cried and tried to embrace Velma, but the smell of booze and lavender perfume repulsed her.

"Did I hear free wine being served?"

Jessica ignored the question, "Now, you sit down right here." At a distance, Jessica thought to herself.

Velma seemed to fully wakeup once the early morning breeze hit her face.

"I can't believe I fell asleep here, oh, I'm so embarrassed."

Jessica wondered if she had really been here all night or had killed her husband and passed out here after a murderous rage.

"Oh, you slept here all night? Well, it was— is a beautiful morning. It's funny, I thought I saw you a couple of hours ago… I had writer's block and went for a walk on the lower deck and thought I saw you sneaking around." Jessica lied.

Fear played on Velma's face like a late-night movie.

"You must be mistaken."

"No, I don't think so. Your signature color gives you away, my dear."

"So, I'm the only person in the world who wears lavender? Well, I don't know how you got so famous, Mrs. Fletcher but something tells me you must have jumped in bed with the right people to get where you are."

Jessica's eyes flared. She hated sex and according to her dear departed husband Frank, she was frigid. For someone to even imply that she used feminine ways to get somewhere was a hurtful thing.

"I'm sorry you have to belittle other people to make yourself feel tall. I wanted to be gentle with you because I came to tell you some upsetting news. Now that I see you are fully awake; I must tell you. Your husband, Captain Gist, is dead. Murdered in his sleep."

"Velma took a moment for the words to register and stared a Jessica as if she was speaking a language she didn't understand."

"I'm sorry." Jessica did mean it. She wasn't a fan of the man; he was mean and a sex manic, but this woman had loved him once.

"No! ... no!" Velma screamed as the ocean water became rough around the boat. It was almost like the sea was reacting to Velma's rage. Jessica had to hold on as the ship shook back and forth.

Jessica tried to grab Velma's hand, but the hysterical woman had jumped up and started moving away by holding on to the tip of deck chairs that were lined in a neat row. She would learn later they were bolted to the floor for situations like this.

"Oh, dear, Velma, you could hurt yourself."

An open package of peanut M&M's fell out of Velma's pocket, sending the colored candy rolling down the boat as it rocked. The chocolate treat had distracted Jessica and when she turned back to the hysterical woman, Velma had removed all of her clothes and was standing by the deck, looking over at the wild sea.

Jessica's first thought was; age could be cruel to a woman's breast. Poor Velma's once perky bosom was now resting under her arms, a terrible look when you're staring at the back of someone.

"I can't live now," Velma screamed to the sea, "Who will smack my face and call me by another woman's name?"

Jessica rolled her eyes and tried walking by holding the lounge chairs the same way Velma had. Water was splashing on the deck so hard both women were wet and the floor slippery. Jessica tripped and fell back and almost overboard. When she steadied her feet and looked over at Velma, she covered her mouth in horror. Velma was climbing over the railing. Age hadn't been kind to the woman's backside either.

"Please, don't do this, think of your son— your granddaughter."

Velma jumped off the deck and made a splash in the water. Jessica took a couple of minutes to maneuver her way over to where Velma disappeared.

"Man! I mean—woman overboard!"

Crew members in pressed white clothes marched up to the deck. Some were already lowering lifeboats after Jessica explained what happened. The sea had settled as Jessica peered over into the water. Where was Velma?

"Trouble seems to follow you, Mrs. Fletcher."

Jessica turned around from the ugly scene with her hair blowing wildly. A quick adjustment from the turquoise scarf that was around her neck had her hair held perfectly in place. Mr. McCree's red hair stood on its ends, and he didn't seem to mind. He was not amused to be kept waiting.

"Grooming for the press? Maybe turn this story into one of your tawdry books? You know, I read once that most writers were mistreated by their parents and spent the rest of their lives writing stories in a feeble attempt to get the darkness out of their hearts."

Jessica smiled and tried not to roll her large, lovely eyes. In truth, she had a perfect childhood with loving parents and was not going to be analyzed by anybody who couldn't use a hair conditioner.

"Oh, really? I read a good article once as well, it said most detectives went into the field because they were only good at working with the lowlifes of society and not real people."

Mr. McCree had to close his mouth with his hand. He chose to ignore her comment. "What happened?"

"I was casually talking with her and thought I could break the tragedy to her gently."

"Yes, and you drove her over the edge. How do I know what you even said to Velma? Maybe you pushed her?"

"And stayed on the top deck yelling for people to come save her? I think you can't believe that."

Mr. McCree didn't answer but his face answered for him. He didn't think Jessica pushed Velma off the boat, maybe not physically. If they can recover her body, they can test how she fell off. If Jessica Fletcher did assist in making Velma jump, that would be another story.

He was starting to think the sea air had finally done him in. Why would this middle-aged woman care to hurt Velma? She was just another nosy woman, living for the thrill of gossip and a story to take back to her bridge club.

Still, he didn't trust this woman. On the surface, she was an easy-going teacher-turned mystery writer. He had a feeling, like a rock stuck in your shoe and he couldn't figure it out until he shook his foot.

Under her wholesome looks lay something dark, something evil, something bought from Forever 21.

He felt determined to find out what it was or die trying.

As Mr. McCree went on one of the lifeboats into the water. Jessica looked around the deck and was about to give up until she saw a small rope hanging off the deck that led into the water. The rope was about ten feet from where Velma jumped. The rope was cut with something with a jagged edge. Why was this here? There was also a window underneath where she jumped. Did Velma simply slip into the window? It looked locked from what she could see but, she could have closed it afterward.

Then it came to her; the rope could be something else altogether. Had someone used this to sneak off the ship after killing Captain Gist? Another spurned lover perhaps?

Fabian watched Jessica from afar as she looked over the scene. When he joined her, Jessica noted that his smile seemed evil. She also thought it odd how he stared down into the water like a cat on a window ledge. How much was Fabian willing to risk falling off?

"This seawater is like love, happy and calm like it is now and other times, roaring and horrific."

Jessica ignored his comment, "I'm curious about that window there. Did anyone check it?"

Fabian had to lean over to see it, "Oh, yes. You don't think she slipped in there? But why; to make everyone feel sorry for her?"

Jessica didn't answer his questions, "It's worth a look."

As they took the elevator down, Jessica wet her lips and took a deep breath. "Did they find her?" Jessica knew the obvious answer if he was checking the window but still, she had to ask.

"Sorry, but she's part of the sea now." He laughed crudely and stopped himself when Jessica raised her eyebrows. "I'm sorry, Mrs. Fletcher but I'm not going to pretend to mourn a woman who was so rude to me and had the personality of a roach."

Jessica coughed, "Do you blame her? I'm sorry, Fabian but you were having an affair with her husband. Some women would have murdered you."

Jessica's comment was meant to shock, and Fabian fell for it. "I think that's why she came on this ship, to murder me. I found her this morning with her ear to my door."

"Oh? And did you confront her?"

"No, I was coming down the hall and just backed away, she never saw me but I'm sure she was trying to see if I was in there with her husband."

Jessica thought the Captain must have been visiting Jula's room. Something Jula probably didn't tell Mr. McCree.

The room under where Velma jumped was a storage area. Furniture and other supplies littered the room. Jessica went to the window and wiped the cobwebs around the frame. It was also padlocked from the inside.

"Satisfied now? That window probably hasn't been open in years."

Both their eyes went to the chair under the window.

"I'm not satisfied, far from it. This chair has been used recently." Jessica moved the chair a little and then back into place.

"Oh, fabulous! This is just how your inspector character speaks in your newest book, Bloody Ballet."

As Jessica gave him a look, he went on. "But you'll have to work a little harder, J. B. Some of the maids come in here to rest and smoke the devil's cigarette—that's right, marijuana. I warned them not to, but I have to catch them puffing the stuff before I can report them."

The little guy was right, there was no way Velma could have come into the room without messing up all the dust on the window. Would they ever find her body? The thought was more gruesome than an elderly Russian guy in a thong.

As Jessica went down the see-through steps, she took note of her friend, Sweetie, in the corner, wearing dark sunglasses. Odd that she didn't come over after everything that happened to support or maybe inquire about her soon-to-be mother in law.

Very odd indeed.

Rob pounded on the painted wood but his daughter, Twinkles wouldn't answer the bathroom door. His daughter took the liberty to decorate her the door with twenty or so stars. Luckily, his mother was married to Captain Gist, or he'd have to pay for the damage.

A soft knock at the cabin door startled him. He slipped the pill bottle that stood on top of the dresser into a half-closed dresser drawer and answered it, expecting his fiancé, Sweetie.

Rob's expression changed as he saw Jessica Fletcher standing there. It was early in the morning, and he wondered what the old gal was up to. He had a good idea. Women found him irresistible.

"I'm sorry to bother you but I just had to come." Jessica walked in without being asked and scanned the room. "This is such a tragedy, and my sorrow goes out to you and your daughter." Jessica noticed the dresser drawer half-open. What did he hide in their so quickly?

"Thank you, Mrs. Fletcher. It was a shock for all of us and I still don't know how we will get through it. Twinkles has decided to work on a dance number in honor of the tragedy."

That should increase the pain, "How nice... Is Sweetie okay?"

"My beloved took the news hard and needed to rest. As you know she's such a sheltered thing. Murder usually only happens in movies and books and not real life.

Not true, most people were just oblivious. Jessica also took notice of all the framed photos of Twinkles. Odd to travel with all of this. The little brat was seen in various sexy poses not fitting a young girl. In her day—as old as it made her feel to think this way—in her day, if a young girl wanted her cheeks rouged with pink, her mother would give her a good slapping.

Rob smiled when he saw Jessica looking at the photos. She was a famous author, maybe her connections could help his daughter become a star.

"Oh, look at your daughter here, tap dancing in a graveyard, and, oh! and this one, roller-skating and smoking a cigarette... in a bikini?"

"I know what you're thinking, and don't worry, Mrs. Fletcher, she doesn't inhale."

Jessica's eyes deceived her, and she fought hard not to roll them by turning again to the photos. She took note that not one photo showed his fiancé and her friend, Sweetie. Very bizarre for a soon-to-be-married couple.

"My daughter is a great singer, actress, model. She's also a world-known baton champ."

The glitter and blood-covered baton poking out of Captain Gist's chest flashed before her eyes.

"Maybe, she could even write books like you…"

"Yes, I'm sure she could do anything her little heart wanted. I just have to ask—out of writer's curiosity, where were you and your daughter last night after midnight when Captain Gist retired?"

"Excuse me? Do you mean when Captain Gist was killed? Oh, Mrs. Fletcher, I'll forgive your wicked mind. I was in bed dreaming of my honeymoon and my darling daughter was asleep, dreaming of princesses and unicorns."

Jessica wondered why Rob suddenly forgot about his 'darling daughter' taking a mysterious walk.

"Hey, poop breath, where is my retainer?" Twinkles yelled through the bathroom door.

Rob frowned and gave Jessica a weak smile, "It's in your Barbie suitcase, dear."

"It better be or else."

Jessica thought about what the spoiled kid meant. Was this just a bratty, yet normal girl or did she mean something more threatening? Was the pintsized minx capable of stabbing her baton through a grown man's chest? And taking on her father? She couldn't picture that unless Captain Gist was already sleeping thanks to being drugged. Twinkles was also a so-called baton champ and probably could spin that stick until the cats came home.

"Kids today."

"Indeed... I'm really sorry about your mother. Did she talk of suicide before?" Jessica asked with genuine interest.

"Mother? No, you must be confused. It was Captain Gist that got murdered."

Jessica covered her mouth in shock. The poor sap didn't know his mother jumped to her death over half an hour ago. "I'm so sorry, I thought you knew. Your mother jumped off the top deck about twenty minutes ago. I tried to stop her but before I knew it, she jumped. Captain Gist's murder was too much for her."

"Both of them are dead? This is a nightmare; I can't believe it." Rob's tears seemed real.

Jessica gave Rob several minutes to get himself together. The man was an ugly crier and she tried not to stare until he picked himself off the floor, "I know this is hard, and excuse me for saying this, but do you think Velma jumped out of guilt for killing Captain Gist."

Rob looked shocked and then like a light went on in his head. I honestly don't know, but that red-headed devil, Mr. McCree thinks Twinkles killed Captain Gist. Someone was trying to frame her! Please tell me this is all a joke. And not so close to when my daughter is poised to become a superstar.

Jessica found his behavior unusual and wondered if Rob killed his stepfather. She was about to pry more when loud knocking came on their cabin door.

Mr. McCree was standing outside with a few crew members dressed in crisp white uniforms. Though the men looked sharp their tired faces betrayed them. With one murder and now a suicide, the men probably didn't have much sleep.

"I'm sorry, son, but I have to tell you something." Mr. McCree said

"Thank you but Mrs. Fletcher here has already informed me of mother's passing."

"Oh, has she? Mrs. Fletcher! You seem to have your nose all over this ship."

Rob became angry. "How dare you speak to a star that way!"

Jessica was a celebrity, but few people recognized her, and she was far from a star. "It's okay Rob."

"I don't think it is. I was sitting here having my cornflakes when I should have been informed right away that my mother leapfrogged off this vessel! Oh, mother! My mother is dead!" Rob threw himself at Mr. McCree and the ship's head of security looked uncomfortable.

"Maybe, he needs a doctor?" Jessica asked but everyone ignored her. Rob was now in hysterics, demanding to see where his mother jumped.

"They'll be plenty of time for that after some questions," Mr. McCree said.

"You can go question a shark! Show me where my mother did herself in! Oh, she must have killed Captain Gist and the pain was too much. Oh, now I have to worry about picking out a coffin."

Soon it was determined to just take Rob to where Velma jumped and shut him up. You couldn't blame him; his mother did just commit suicide but there was still something in the way he was acting that made Jessica question his grief.

When they were gone, Jessica thought she would snoop around before she went to look for Sweetie. Her friend could not marry into this sort of family, no matter how desperate she was to get married.

Jessica pulled open the drawer that was half open and studied the pillbox. The pills were prescribed to Sweetie and were used for severe cases of insomnia. Why did Rob have it? Were they used to drug Captain Gist to make him easier to kill? It was something she was determined to find out. The thought that Sweetie had used the pills to drug Captain Gist herself and kill him entered her mind at an alarming rate.

"Get your filthy paws off my dad's underwear, you pervert!"

The upturned mouth of Twinkles stood in the doorway with her hands on her hips.

"It's not what you think," Jessica said, sounding rather guilty.

"Yeah, right. Like this isn't the first time a senior citizen was hot for my dad's boxer shorts. I'm about to scream for help, tell me a good reason why I shouldn't."

Jessica's eyes doubled in size, and she clutched her heart. Maybe this was the end of her rather double life.

Chapter Seven

"Your father asked me to tell you the news." Jessica lied. "I'm afraid he's taken it hard. It's rather shocking. Maybe we should go for ice cream first."

"I don't eat sugar when it's audition season, so spit it out, old lady."

Jessica had never met a child who was as vicious as this one. It's almost like she wasn't a child at all and a bitter old woman.

"I'm sorry but your grandmother has committed suicide."

Twinkles spit on the ground, "So, she finally did it."

"Oh? Velma talked of suicide before?"

"Yes. She was depressed about her life, her husband, the kind of salad dressing to buy at the store."

When Twinkles ignored her and started dancing, Jessica felt her blood pressure rising. Playing nice with this glittery brat was a waste of time.

"Don't worry your dear heart about her soul. Killing herself might not get her into heaven but at least she'll end up in a nice warm place."

Twinkles almost cracked a smile, "That's a good one, Jess."

Only Jessica's good friends called her 'Jess' and this little demon seed was more foe than friend. Insulting her would be of no use when she had no heart.

"I'm sorry, child. Can I get you a glass of milk?"

Twinkle's lit a cigarette and blew smoke into Jessica's direction. Telling her that she was in a NO SMOKING cabin would be a waste of time.

"I heard your grandfather—"

111

"—step-grandfather!" Twinkles grumbled.

"Your step-grandfather was kicking you and your father off the ship. That must have been painful for you."

"Ha! I only came aboard this floating tuna can because daddy is getting married, again. and he told me I'd get a chance to perform."

"Oh, your father has been married before?"

"Many times!"

Jessica excused herself, though the child didn't seem to notice as she was doing some type of ballet split on the floor. Jessica felt she needed to warn Sweetie; this family had more nuts in it than San Francisco.

Jessica ran right into Sweetie on the deck.

"Oh, Oh, Sweetie, are you alright?"

"Jessica! Oh, I can't believe all of this disturbing news and now Rob is under the ship's doctor's care. He's distraught over his mother's death and almost jumped where she did."

They sat down by the nearly abandoned pool bar and Jessica ordered Sweetie the strongest alcoholic drink the bartender could make.

As sweetie poured out her heart, Jessica thought about Rob, he didn't seem so upset about his mother's death at first. Some people acted differently when bad news happens. She couldn't put her finger on it but there was something in front of her face, but what?

Jessica joined Sweetie into staring at two women jumping into the pool. At first glance, they looked like twins with the same figure, haircut and bathing suits that had bananas on them. If you looked at them long enough, you realized they weren't twins, just two whackos who dressed alike. It made her think; nothing is ever what it seems to be most of the time.

"Oh, Jessica, what am I going to do. Rob and I were to be married tonight on the upper deck when the full moon came into view."

"How could you possibly know if there is going to be a full moon?"

"Oh, it was Rob, he planned the whole thing. Looked it up somehow when we first boarded."

"Did he? How romantic."

"But now everything is like egg salad left too long in a car—spoiled. I'm not returning the wedding gifts; I can tell you that—"

Jessica's raised eyebrows made Sweetie soften her face.

"I feel bad about the Captain, even though I didn't know him and Rob's mother, even though she seemed like a vampire just waiting to suck the life out of our future happiness."

"She did seem a bit... high strung."

"Oh, Jess, I'll admit it," Sweetie said, staring into an empty glass. "God forgive me, but I'm glad the bitch is dead."

Jessica's thoughts went to Rob's rude daughter, and she took a large gulp of her nearly full drink.

"Maybe, you should delay the wedding, until everything gets straightened out."

"I can't, Jessica, you don't understand."

Jessica thought she understood. Rob was unlike anyone Sweetie ever came into contact with. He was wild, unpredictable and mysterious. He probably also made love to her like a madman, something Sweetie had only read about in the many books she read. Now she was stuck; should she go back to her boring life with her cat and take-out food and only read about excitement in romance novels or stay with Rob and live it.

After ordering cherry Jell-O-shots for them, Sweetie admitted to much of everything Jessica thought about her situation except one shocker.

She was pregnant.

"And you're drinking alcohol? No more for you, Jessica said and ordered the bartender to take the empty glasses and give them some mint tea."

"Oh, Jess, my mother had a glass of wine every night when pregnant with me and look how great I turned out!" Sweetie stood up, dropped her skirt, revealing a green swimsuit and dived into the pool, scaring the two skinny women swimmers.

"Oh, cupcakes with sprinkles! Please, Sweetie, be careful!"

"Come join us! The water is warm!"

"No thanks, I haven't shaved above my ankles in years. Please, just be careful, you're with child!"

"Ha! I love drinking pool water!"

"Oh, my, please, Sweetie! oh, dear."

Sweetie stepped out of the pool and Jessica wrapped a large towel around her.

"Thanks. And you're wrong."

"Oh?"

"Yes, It's not child, it's children. I'm having triplets!"

"Oh!" Jessica stood up and jumped headfirst into the pool, splashing the two lookalike skinny women.

As Jessica swam on her back, spitting out water, she noticed various suspects around the area looking guiltier than a dog who just ate the pot roast off the kitchen table.

Standing on the deck overlooking the pool stood Fabian, working on his tablet and looking around suspiciously. His neck brace was now decorated with mini fake diamonds. When Jessica caught his eye, he looked away but not before the sun made a beam of light flare off his diamonds, it almost blinded her.

"Oh, Jess, are you sure you don't want to go change into a bathing suit," Sweetie asked.

"No. dear. I'm fine. I need to think about the murder of Captain Gist and the water will help me think."

"Oh, you writers, always working." Sweetie thought Jessica was strange to swim in a pantsuit but who was she to judge? She took bubble baths while eating mayonnaise sandwiches.

Jessica did a backflip and saw Twinkles, blowing bubbles and twirling her baton. The tiny-terror must have a suitcase full of them. When Twinkles saw Jessica, she spit a huge wad of gum into the pool and turned up her nose. Soon her father came and joined her. From what Jessica could tell, they arguing. Soon, Rob walked off without even going over to Sweetie, luckily her friend had closed her eyes.

Jula was speaking to some passengers and letting her weird eyes roam the deck. She wore guilt like her pushup bra; hidden but painfully obvious.

As Jessica sipped a frozen mojito on a lounge chair next to Sweetie, she started to wonder about two things; the murder and mixing so many different kinds of alcohol. The question of who killed Sal ran through her mind for the half-hour she'd been in the pool. For a while, she almost left her friend out of the picture.

"Now that Captain Gist is dead and his wife committed suicide, did you decide to forgo the wedding for now?" Jessica asked, sipping her drink and getting a brain freeze.

"Oh, no, Jess. Rob asked me to get married tonight. He's devastated by his mother becoming fish food but knows we shouldn't stop our happiness. His mother would want that."

Jessica didn't want to remind her what Velma had said about the wedding or her. Was her friend just desperate to get married or was she hiding a sinister lust to kill? A lust

Jessica understood, and the feeling was another reason she could always pry out the truth from people keeping secrets. She was keeping a huge secret and no; it wasn't her famous clam chowder recipe either.

"I'm surprised Mr. McCree is letting the wedding happen."

"Well, it was a hard sell, I'll admit but when we threatened to send Twinkles in to dance for him, he relented."

Jessica raised her eyebrows, "Oh? Well, I guess he's not fond of dance."

"We're not getting into port until mid-morning, so it's best to have our fun now. Once the local authorities boarded the ship, we will be interviewed and who knows, we'll all get thrown into some foreign prison with foul-smelling soap."

"Oh, dear. You may be right."

Sweetie rubbed her arms as if she had goose-pimples, "Of course, Velma killed him, but they'll want to pin it on one of us because they can't prosecute a dead person... It will be a horror, we will be starved and forced to wear dungarees until one of us admit to the murder."

Jessica gave Sweetie a look, her friend had some imagination, though if she thought about it, she probably wasn't far off. This is why she had to solve the murder before the ship docked in Santorini. If not, she could be stuck in the Greek Islands for months and if would be a shame to miss Cabot Cove's annual pig naming contest in June.

"If Velma didn't kill him, aren't you scared to be on the ship with a murderer running wild."

If Jessica thought she could scare Sweetie, she was wrong. Her friend from New York just rolled her eyes and patted her knee.

"Oh, Jess. I would have thought you figured it out already. Like I said before, Velma did murder her husband and jumped the plank afterward out of guilt."

Jessica wanted that to be true but something in her gut told her it wasn't Velma. Hopefully, it wasn't just gas.

"Suicide victims that murder someone will usually confess their crimes before killing themselves."

Sweetie took her nose out of her bride magazine and for once looked terrified, "Oh, tuna. If that's true I could be getting married to a bloodthirsty fiend on board this ship. If he—"

"—or she," Jessica added.

"Oh, Jess, you still act like a teacher. Okay. If he or she does kill again, I pray to Jesus that they wait until we cut the wedding cake."

Chapter Eight

Jessica put down the ship's free phone and slipped the pill bottle into her pocket. She had paid a visit to Rob's room to borrow it. By the pool, Sweetie had told her that she lost her sleeping pills somehow and dreaded trying to fall asleep on her own tonight.

Why did Rob have her pills? Was it to drug Captain Gist to make him easier to kill or had Sweetie devilishly did the murder herself and planted the drugs in Rob's drawer to frame him? She wasn't sure.

Talking to Seth made her homesick for Cabot Cove; who cares if it was the hidden murder capital of the world? No thanks to her but from her viewpoint, a couple hundred of murders were justified. Sometimes she had dreams where she was a human, walking bottle of dish cleaning liquid, ridding the earth of the greasiest and grimiest people.

Jessica walked a little and smiled at a young couple until they started doing things with their tongues that made her think of a dog licking himself. The humidity of the day was now turning into a lovely evening. The soft breeze was trying its hardest to penetrate her hair to no avail.

As she suspected, the prescription was for a powerful knockout drug that only was to be taken before bed. Seth mentioned they were highly addictive.

Seth also said that if you took a lot of this sleeping drug it would make you erratic, even suicidal. Had Rob been slipping these pills to Captain Gist and even his own mother? If that was fact, he had a hand in Velma's death as well.

The fact that Sweetie slept through the whole night of the murder made her wonder as well. Did he drug his fiancé, so he could go kill the already drugged Captain?

And why did he do it? The Captain was no fan of Rob or his daughter's performing ability. Would a grown man kill somebody for that? If he thought Captain Gist stood in the way of his daughter's fame, he might. Rob seemed rather possessed by the fact of making his kid famous. The thought that he was just marrying Sweetie to get her money and kill her entered her mind at an alarming rate. With Sweetie's money, he would have even more resources to make his brat a teen sensation.

Lord, help us all.

"Talking to yourself again, Mrs. Fletcher?" Mr. McCree's voice rattled her nerves and she looked up sharply. There was something creepy about the man that she couldn't put her finger on, but if she did, she'd use hand sanitizer right after.

"You have a very bad habit of surprising people."

"I'll keep that in mind. I suppose you're going to be part of this charade tonight—the wedding?"

"My friend wants to continue her plans. I can't blame her for that. Did you ever recover anything of poor Velma?"

Mr. McCree lit a cigarette, "I hope you don't mind."

She did mind, "Velma is really dead then?"

"I'm afraid so unless she's a mermaid. I think she killed her husband because of his numerous affairs."

"Interesting theory," smiled Jessica. "And then jumped overboard without as much as a sorry? I don't think so, Mr. McCree. For the short time, I knew Velma, she was a dirty boozer, yes, but no shrinking violet. She surprised her husband aboard this ship to tell him she was getting a divorce. A move she could have done over the phone. No, she came in-person to embarrass him one last time. She was far from suicidal."

Mr. McCree's face betrayed his earlier confidence. He threw his lit cigarette overboard, a move that made Jessica angry.

"That pollutes the sea."

"I'm sorry, Mrs. Fletcher. I'm also sorry for what I'm about to ask you. I think you know who killed Captain Gist."

Jessica's laugh wasn't joyous, "I have an idea and I'm going to need your help."

***

Though most people aboard Seamen's Delight looked scared, drunk or bored. Sweetie ignored them as she stood at the beginning of the flower-covered walkway waiting for her wedding music to be played.

In her mind, she had waited years—too many years—to be asked for her hand in marriage and this was her time to shine. Murder, suicide or the bad crab cakes she had last night wasn't going to stop her from being Mrs. Sweetie Pye.

Waiting on the sidelines was Jessica, dressed in a pale-yellow pantsuit. She wondered where the groom was. Maybe just the wedding day jitters? She wasn't so sure. When no one was looking she made a beeline out of the ballroom and downstairs to where Rob's cabin was.

The hallway that his cabin was on was long, narrow and dimly lit. She had a feeling someone took all the lightbulbs out of the fixtures. Was a fiend waiting in the shadows to jump out and murder her like she'd done so many times herself?

Jessica laughed and pulled out her nunchucks. One of her many talents—and they were endless—was martial arts. She'd been taught by David Hu in San Francisco's Chinatown when she murdered a notorious madam by the name of May Wank. After she framed an awful Chinese gangster for the madam's murder, Detective Hu thanked her by teaching her how to use the traditional Okinawan martial arts weapon, which consisted of two sticks connected at one end by a short chain or rope.

In most states, nunchucks were illegal because they can cause serious injury or death. Luckily, no one ever thought to check a middle-aged mystery writer from Maine for deadly weapons. She never left home without them.

Jessica swung her pink nunchucks around with quick movements. The sweet-looking white daisies on the deadly weapons were a nice touch. If some sicko was waiting in the wings for her, he or she would be coleslaw when she was through with them.

Jessica took a deep breath and practiced her nunchucks between her legs with movements that would make Bruce Lee blush. As she went down the dark hallway with her yellow purse around her neck, Jessica swung her weapons in every direction possible.

When she thought she heard footsteps behind her, she swung around, and no one was there and lowered her weapon. With a sigh, she turned around just as a mysterious person jumped out and grabbed her. As they struggled, Jessica tried to look at the face of her assailant, but the light was too dim.

When Jessica got her bearings, she had her nunchucks around the mystery person's neck so fast; they hit the ground before they knew what was happening.

The quick movement made Jessica fall back into the narrow wall. As she composed herself, the mystery person got up and ran down the hall. If only she'd seen the face. For some reason, she thought it was a man because the hands were so rough.

When she got to Rob's door, it was half-open.

The room looked like it had been ransacked and smelled like fish. Jessica wondered if she was imagining things, how could she smell fish? The window was closed and there were no food dishes. Fresh footprints and what looked like droplets of blood led to the bathroom.

No one was in there.

What was going on here? Had Rob been hurt, killed or kidnapped? She'd have to inform Mr. McCree and poor Sweetie, pregnant and left at the altar.

Sweetie?

The alarming thought came into her mind as quickly as the buzz from a good Bloody Mary. Had she killed Rob and went on to her wedding, ready to play the jilted bride to the hilt until his body was discovered? And why kill him? By all means, she adored the man, even with that dancing devil daughter as a soon-to-be stepchild from hell.

Or was it the fact that Rob has been married three times already? And was known in New York to be a male gold-digger? Jessica got the information this morning from a friend in New York, who also informed her that one of Rob's wives died from mysterious circumstances as well. Maybe Sweetie found this out and realized he was only using her and decided to kill him?

Before she even left the room, Mr. McCree entered it.

"I suppose you get a gold star."

Jessica pretended something was stuck on her shoe. "I only said Rob could disappear. I had no idea when."

"So, I guess we are to assume he's been either killed or kidnapped?"

"Yes, and such a shame on his wedding day."

In the hallway, Fabian listened, turned and left.

***

When the DJ cued her wedding music, Sweetie wet her pink stained lips and felt gorgeous. The only negative was her sinuses. Her head was throbbing, and hearing was hard because her ears were so clogged up with pressure. No matter, she had dreamed of this day since a young girl and nothing or no one was going to ruin it.

Sweetie had demanded a long walk down the aisle and got one. She was to walk a curved aisle that went around the ballroom and up the stairs to the top deck. The priest and Rob would be waiting for her, both impressed with how classy and lovely she was.

The DJ gave her the go with his thumb. She was so happy that she blocked out all of the faces and sounds of the room. This was her moment to shine, and she was going to take her time walking and showing off her untraditional teal wedding dress and matching veil.

Sweetie kept her nose up high and only caught the sounds from clapping and cries of joy from the crowd as she went down the flower-covered aisle. The women aboard were most definitely jealous of her, she was positive. From the blurs around her, she could tell everyone was excited and she felt like a movie star. When she got to the stairs, Sweetie stopped to pose and wave to her public before going further.

This was the best day of her life and she had fault hard to wide up here. She felt almost like she was floating like an angel, a beautiful teal angel.

The only thing that brought her back to earth was the unmistakable sounds of laughter. Sweetie thought she was imaging things and continued her strut.

As she glided up the floral and lace decorated stairs, she couldn't shake the feeling that something was amiss. Sweetie finally realized something was wrong when she saw the priest and he was smiling weirdly.

All of a sudden, her ears and eyes were open, and the room was spinning. The wedding guests weren't cheering and jealous, they were laughing at her. The dumb DJ was playing a popular Halloween song instead of the traditional wedding song she gave him.

"He did the mash, he did the monster mash. The monster mash, it was a graveyard smash…"

She had been preening and strutting down the aisle to a Halloween song like The Bride of Frankenstein instead of a dainty bride.

"You idiot! That's the wrong song!" she waved her fist down to the clueless DJ.

Jessica and Mr. McCree came into the ballroom just as the laughing was dying down until The Monster Mash was abruptly cut off and the traditional wedding march came on the speakers. This song seemed to make the guests laugh again and even louder.

Sweetie lifted her dress and jumped the last two steps to where the priest was standing with his bible over his mouth.

Downstairs where the guests stood, a huge wedding cake was wheeled out and everyone looked confused.

"Oh, goodness no. Sweetie has decided to go on with the wedding and no groom, how terrible," Jessica said.

"And it looks like everybody has come to see her desperate act," Mr. McCree added.

A drunk man came over to the cake, "When are we cutting her up?"

"Hey, take that wedding cake away!" Mr. McCree yelled at the two men, but they ignored him because they were staring up at Sweetie. Jessica and Mr. McCree followed the eyes.

"—And by the power invested in me, I pronounce you man and wife."

Sweetie and Rob kissed, and everyone downstairs clapped wildly.

Jessica and Mr. McCree looked at each other in shock and then around at the other party guests.

"I'll be back." Mr. McCree went over to one of his men.

Jessica clapped but searched the crowd and it made her eyes heavy. There were too many people stuffed into the ballroom and upper deck overlooking it. Sweetie and Rob posed for pictures with the still-smiling priest.

"Had too many drinks, Mrs. Fletcher?"

Jessica blinked and ignored her comment, "Hello, Jula. I'm surprised to see you here."

"I know but I do have a job to do, even something morbid as celebrating with a bunch of people, one being the psycho killer who ended my man's life."

Jessica wrinkled her nose, "You sound bitter—"

"Duh."

"—I know it's been tough but you're still young enough to enjoy life. Mourn yes, but don't let your anger control your life."

"And what do you know? When was last time you had a good roll in the sheets?"

Jessica's lip trembled but she held her stiff smile, "by the looks of it, dearie, you've spent your adult life rolling in the sheets and are you any happier than me? I don't think so. Sex and passion are great, but love and feelings are what last a lifetime. Try it."

"Go tell it to a church!" Jula stormed through the crowd and Jessica laughed.

Above Sweetie and Rob was a glass roof that had been opened and the stars in the sky were magnificent to view, almost like you could reach out and touch them.

Mr. McCree came over after witnessing Jula's outburst, "Who put her batteries in? So, my men have been watching Rob, he was getting a shave and a haircut when no one couldn't find him."

"The whole time?"

"They didn't leave him for a second."

"Then, what was all that in his room?"

"I have no idea and will interview him about it. As you can see, I can't do much now."

Jessica had a sick feeling that it was Mr. McCree who attacked her in the hallway. Was he the killer after all? She wasn't sure.

Sweetie and Rob came to the balcony overlooking the ballroom as everyone screamed and clapped and cheered. A few still giggling.

The large cake was just directly under them and was lit with 37 candles—the number of days they dated before Rob proposed.

"Thank you all for witnessing our love," Sweetie said, waving at the guests like she was Evita.

"Thank you all for coming and I'm sorry fella's, she's all mine now," Rob added to cheers and a few chuckles about The Monster Mash.

As the newly married couple tongue kissed like messy teenagers, a body fell passed them and on the wedding cake. Just then The Monster Mash music blasted on again—the DJ had hit the wrong button again.

Jessica wiped the icing from her eyes so she could see. Mr. McCree slipped and fell. He took a good two minutes trying to balance himself on the slippery floor before he could stand.

The place erupted in chaos and most people ran from the room. When Jessica and Mr.

McCree came over to check the body, they were both stunned to see it was Velma.

Chapter Nine

"Is she dead?" Jessica asked.

"Yes, I'm afraid she is, and this is a fresh wound on her head."

Jessica looked closely, "I'm not a doctor but there is no way she's been floating in the sea this whole time." Jessica made a face like she smelled something bad."

"Sorry about that, I had the seven-bean burrito for breakfast."

Jessica rolled her eyes, "No, not that. It's the fish smell again."

"We are on the water."

Jessica went through Velma's wet pockets, "Yes! Look at this."

"You shouldn't touch the body!"

Jessica opened her fist and showed two small dead multicolored fish. "I doubt she hoped to use these as currency in the next port."

Mr. McCree tried not to smile, "But what would they be doing in her pockets? I can't believe she's been dead all this time and shows up now with mini fish in her pocket."

"I think she was killed maybe an hour or so ago and the fish were put there to make us believe they were from the sea. I also remember these fish. There is a huge tank when you first come on the ship, right by where passengers have the option of getting a picture taken."

"Oh, you're right but the killer can't be that stupid to think I would fall for that."

Jessica raised an eyebrow but went on, "This whole affair has been a solid try by an amateur, to confuse, engage and trick us into believing all kinds of things. I think I know now who the killer is, I just have to make some phone calls."

Mr. McCree looked worried, "You thought you knew before, and you failed like Hilary Clinton."

Jessica didn't like her sleuthing skills questioned by a boat detective and let her temper show, "I'm sorry you feel that way, but you haven't had one solid idea from when this whole tragedy started."

"I'm—I'm sorry. I'm used to cases like, jewelry being stolen or passengers dying from bad rice pudding, but cold-blooded murder is something new for me."

"Not for me. Now, let's work on a plan to trap a killer."

**

The wedding went on and was an elaborate affair when it came to the food and drinks. A rather dim-witted waiter had managed to scoop up parts of the wedding cake not crushed by Velma's fall and serve it to the guests. Only one drunk guy seemed to enjoy the dessert.

Seated at the main dining table reserved for the wedding party sat Jessica, touching up her lipstick. When she was done, she yawned loudly and looked around at all the suspects.

"Oh, Jess, you must be exhausted at your age?" Sweetie asked.

Jessica blinked, "I am. I got a disturbing phone call from my friend, Dan Singer. He's retired from the FBI, but still has connections."

"Is it something about my father—and now mother's murder?" Rob asked, looking more anxious than sad.

"Yes, I'm afraid so."

"Well, spit it out already, old lady, I'm not getting any younger." Twinkles said, blowing a big pink bubble from her mouth. "And I'm bored to death waiting."

"Do not speak to my friend like that. You have to respect older people, young lady," Sweetie added firmly.

"She doesn't mean it, dear. She has stress." Rob patted his wife's knee.

"She's twelve year's old, what the hell can she have to be stressed about?" Sweetie barked and everyone silently agreed with her.

I believe you have some news about the murder, Mrs. Fletcher?" Fabian asked.

All eyes were on Jessica, and she coyly loved being the center of attention. Jessica took her time sipping her tea until she was good and ready to speak.

"Yes, it was quite shocking. Now, I am certain I know who killed Captain Gist and his wife."

"Mind sharing that with me, Mrs. Fletcher?" Mr. McCree asked.

"I'm sorry, but I think it's better if I wait for the local police."

"That's very arrogant of you. Letting us all be on a ship with a crazed killer." Jula added, leaning over a guest.

"The killer is trapped until we get into Santorini. There the local authorities will be waiting for us. Now, I'm sorry but this is for the best. I must lay down before we arrive in two hours, I suggest you all do the same."

Moments after Jessica left, the crowd started to leave as well. After twenty minutes no one was left but the drunk guy eating wedding cake.

***

Jessica pulled the covers up to her nose and her eyes doubled in size. After a moment she realized someone just walked by her cabin and scratched their keys across the door.

How rude, she hated that sound.

After no more sounds, she picked up her book and began reading. This could be a long night, but the killer had only about an hour to kill her before the cruise ship pulled into port. Her eyes felt like weights were attached to the lids and it was a struggle to stay awake.

Jessica awoke without opening her eyes. Her book laid on her chest and she hoped to use it as a weapon. She was pretty sure she knew who the killer was but there was always uncertainty.

Someone was in the room.

As the door closed slowly, she heard the chair by the door being pushed closer to the bed. When the creak of the springs in the chair made noise, Jessica rolled over just in time as the killer's rotisserie skewers pierced the bed.

"Come here—you old suitcase!"

Jessica rolled off the bed and hurt her ankle. The pain was throbbing and shooting up her leg. Unable to walk, Jessica crawled towards the door in agony as Twinkles tried to pull a couple of the skewers free from the mattress.

"Why did you kill your step-grandfather?"

"You're so smart, don't you know?" She spat.

"I know you drugged him at dinner, so you had a better chance of killing him because he was so tall."

Twinkles pulled one skewer from the bed and worked on the next.

"He supported my father, and my father gave me money for my career. He cut us off last week, he didn't know that we knew but his lawyer told us. I wasn't going to let him destroy my career." Another skewer came out of the mattress.

"Why kill your own grandmother?" Jessica was in so much pain but was determined not to die like this and not by the hands of a pre-teen-terror."

Another skewer came loose, "You dummy, my grandmother was in on it but knew they'd blame her first, so she pretended to jump overboard but jumped in the open window underneath, where I was waiting."

"I checked that window; it was bolted shut."

"We sprayed dust and cobwebs on there. It's super amazing stuff, adds an aged look to anything. You can find it in most Halloween stores."

Jessica was at the door and trying to reach the handle, but she couldn't get it. When the first skewer impaled the floor, barely missing her foot, Jessica kicked Twinkles in the face as hard as she could with her good foot. Jessica then rolled over and grabbed the book she was reading. Twinkles looked dazed with a footmark on her face but was crawling and blindly stabbing the floor dangerously close to Jessica.

With all her might, Jessica slapped Twinkles in the face with the book. It knocked her out and sent her backward and across the room.

"That's what you get for saying only losers read books."

The door burst open, and Mr. McCree came into the room with his gun out.

"I can't believe you were right. Kids today!" Mr. McCree said, lowering his gun. "I blame the internet."

"Where were you? I told you to watch my room all night."

"I had to have a bathroom break."

"Did you have the seven-bean burrito again?"

"Right again, Mrs. Fletcher."

Chapter Ten

Jessica plopped into a sun chair, dropping shopping bags by her leg with the bandage. Luckily, her leg wasn't broken but just sprained. Sweetie followed suit next to her and singled to the waiter that they wanted to order.

"Get us something with alcohol, fruit and those paper umbrellas."

"Oh, goodness, Sweetie, it's too early to drink," Jessica laughed.

"Oh, Jess, it's dinner time somewhere in the world, and after everything we've been through, we need it."

"I can't argue with you there. Spending almost two days with the local authorities was a real bore. Luckily, after giving our written statements and Twinkles confessing, they let the ship leave port and finish its destination."

"Yes, and here we are in Mykonos. I must admit I'm still confused about a few things. Like, why did Twinkles kill her step-grandfather and grandmother?"

"Velma and Twinkles planned to kill him together. Most grandmothers spend quality time with their grandkids, but this is ridiculous."

"Remember her bitter face at the local police station? Twinkles gladly confessed to everything but leaving that mysterious hammer that was found in Captain Gist's room."

Jessica coughed, "Some things we will never know..."

"Yeah, like who attacked you outside Rob's door."

Jessica blinked for a moment, "I'm sorry but I just realized something; it was probably Rob. I can see it now—after his haircut, he probably came to his room and saw the blood and knew his devil-daughter was the culprit."

"Rob wouldn't try to hurt you."

"I don't think that he was, I doubt he knew it was his own mother's blood in the room either. Rob is deeply protective of his daughter and was just trying to scare me off so he could wipe up the blood."

"Oh, that is horrible to think of…" Sweetie winched, "So, why did Twinkles kill them?"

"Because with both of them dead, all of the money would go to her father, Rob, who would gladly give her anything she wanted. Twinkles had to do it before Velma and Captain Gist got a divorce."

"I've seen poisonous snakes with better attitudes then that girl. Why did Twinkles kill her grandmother, if she was in on killing Captain Gist?"

Jessica stared at the lethal drink put in front of her and took a sip. She could swear she felt the liquid go through her body like quicksand. Hard liquor was never her favorite but after this cruise, a good buzz was what she needed.

"I think she tricked her grandmother and talked Velma into killing her unfaithful husband. But Twinkles had other plans, she would kill them all."

"So sinful," Sweetie whispered.

"I know, and so young."

"I meant the drink, Jess—but of course, the girl isn't mentally fit to use a hula-hoop, and to think she is my stepdaughter now." Sweetie seemed on the verge of tears.

"So, you're going to remain married to Rob?" Jessica needed another sip to soften the blow of her friend's answer.

"I contacted my lawyer already to get it annulled. I can't blame Rob for loving his daughter but his blindness to what a horrible monster she is—is really a turnoff."

"Sweetie, you're forgetting the triplets."

Sweetie made a pained expression, "Oh, Jess. I went to the ship's doctor, turns out I'm not pregnant at all, just constipated. That's what I get for buying a home pregnancy test at the 99 cents store."

I threw back my head laughing and continued for a good three minutes, much to the embarrassment of Sweetie.

When my phone buzzed in my pocket, I was delighted to see it was Seth. If only he knew how much I cared about him. I'd bet my best turnip pie recipe that the feeling is mutual. I can't risk him ever finding out about my murderous desires.

What would Seth really think if he knew that I kill bad people and frame a person I find annoying for the crime? He probably would reject me and run to the police. Seth is a doctor but that doesn't mean he would understand why I murder people. Sometimes, I don't even know why I do it myself.

For now, I'll keep him at bay. I can't risk him not being in my life if he finds out my dark truth or the fact that I sleep upside down sometimes like a bat.

"Oh, Jess. I just had a horrible thought," Sweetie took a sloppy gulp of her drink. "I'm going to be on the single scene again. I'll miss having a man around the house that doesn't mind cleaning the cat litter."

"I'm sure companionship is up there as well," I said, smiling.

"Don't you ever get lonely? If you don't mind me saying. Dear, dead, Frank, has been gone many years now. There must be someone in your life that makes you want to shave your legs?"

I told my friend that there wasn't. Seth Hazlitt. Cranky. Opinionated and an overachiever and eater was in my thoughts again. I needed to get him off my mind.

Who should I kill next?

Murder, She Tried A Brazilian Wax

Murder, She Wrote parody 2

HUDSON TAYLOR

In need of a juicy book idea, author and jolly serial killer, Jessica Fletcher, travels to Brazil after an old friend pleads for her help. Once in Rio, our gal enters the mysterious Clinica Bonita Agora, run by the elusive Dr. Brimstone. The doctor performs miracles in plastic surgery; so, what if some of his patients wind up disfigured? Of course, wherever Jessica goes, a murder or two are sure to follow.

In this dark-humored adventure, Jessica works overtime to search through the muck of eccentric characters for a victim but also winds up with another murder to solve. As the clock ticks for going under the knife of the creepy doctor, Jessica uses all her tricks-and karate moves in a bid to save the day and leave Brazil with all her original body parts.

On SALE now @Amazon.com

HUDSON TAYLOR

Murder at the Hair Salon

A Golden Girls parody mystery

Who killed obnoxious beauty influencer, Naddie Nuggets, at the hair salon? Better yet, who gave her that stupid name? The list of oddball murder suspects will curl your hair and have you flipping the page when Miami's favorite sassy detectives, Dorothy, Blanche, Rose, and Sophia are on the case.

Who wanted Naddie dead? Was it the ditzy hunk, Chance, who she just dumped? Or maybe it was Sybil, Naddie's beauty influencer competition? How about Mr. George, her former hairdresser, who thought she was a witch, as did her previous hairdresser, Brooks. Maybe it was current hairdresser, Sky, who gave Naddie a hot stone massage she'll never forget. What about greedy hair salon owner, Melody? She seems suspicious. There's also Chance's odd sister, Cassie, who never thought Naddie was good enough for her brother.

On SALE now @Amazon.com

Hudson Taylor

Salsa Hot, Murder Cold

Author of Death of a
Christmas Tree Man

Sal Bunion's attitude was as spicy as his famous salsa. When he turns up dead it's up to sassy Ethel Cunningham to put down the tortilla chips and catch a sick and saucy killer.

Who killed Sal and stole his famous recipe? Maybe his gold obsessed wife Toni, or bitter waitress and girlfriend, Roberta? How about muscular and brooding Pablo? And then there's the mysterious new business partner, Mr. Fox. Did he kill him? Many would think it's one of his estranged children, Sal Jr, Al or Rose.

In a battle of wills, salt and spice, Ethel even has the Clover Court gang of misfit neighbors helping her out in one of her most tricky and tasty mysteries yet.

On SALE now @Amazon.com

After a surprising turn of events, Jolly serial killer, Jessica Fletcher, has decided to get married. Will the groom find out she is more than just a crime-solving mystery novelist?

Murder, She Married Seth

A Murder, She Wrote Parody,

book 3.

Fall 2022